CW00405689

Once Upon
a Christmas Eve

Deborah J Barker

For Beverly and John, who loved Christmas

"The most beautiful experience we can have is the mysterious. It is the fundamental emotion that stands at the cradle of true art and true science."
-Albert Einstein, The World As I See It

Chapter one

Hannah

November 2000

I am born.

The world has been waiting and I am here, at last.

There are some for whom my appearance is the culmination of a long and hopeful vigil. I know nothing of their expectations. My focus is on taking my first breath and negotiating my entry into this cold, startling world.

My future is far from being assured. My parents, oblivious to any destiny that may await their only daughter, have scarcely been bothered by my tardy appearance. To be fair, that they have had to wait a little longer than planned for their second child to emerge into the world, is not down to any whim of mine. Birth has its own plan.

In some ways, it is a miracle that I ever got myself together enough in the first place. My father's lengthy absences (he is a travelling salesman) did not make conception easy. If rumour is to be believed, my parents' union was frowned upon by my maternal grandmother. A travelling salesman whose father had blotted his copy book years before by gazumping my grandparents on the purchase of their very first home, had obstacles aplenty to overcome in winning their approval. But, Hallelujah! I am here.

I am a girl, that much I know. By the look of my mother, I could be round faced and freckled – or are those just the final vestiges of pregnancy that bloat her unremarkable features? I am not smitten by instant love or anything of that sort. I am hungry and looking for food, finding it in her soft, supple nipple, and in the watery, calming liquid that I guzzle like there is no tomorrow. She will squeal in a few hours when I latch on but for now, she is ignorant of what is to come.

My father is conspicuous by his absence. He lies in the same hospital, strapped to a life support machine, two storeys above us, hanging to life by a thread. My mother went into labour when she heard the news. More potent than any induction, the shock of the police woman's words put an end to my apparent reluctance to vacate the womb. Five minutes before she heard, rather than felt the 'pop' that heralded her waters breaking, she had been looking at the Next catalogue and deciding what to buy my father for Christmas. The police woman at the door had waited while she collected herself and then had had to call the ambulance as mother's waters broke in the hall way.

My brother, new from sleep and plump in the way that only three year olds can be, whimpered by her side. Gran came to collect him. We left for the hospital in the ambulance and I managed to stay put until we arrived.

I am swaddled and tucked up in a plastic sided cot. My mother apologises and disappears to see my father. I am left to sleep from the exhaustion of getting here. A comforting, downy darkness envelops me, where the still remembered sounds of the womb play from somewhere in the room.

The first time I see George, the name she calls my father by, he is lying on a hospital bed, with tubes emerging from every part of his body. His head is swathed in bandages and his eyes are closed. He is in an induced coma.

"We have done what we can but he was lying there for some time before anyone found him. We need to do more tests but we believe there could be some brain damage." My mother hears the words and I feel her tremble through my blanket. She holds me out to George,

"Our baby girl, George, see?"

How can he? His eyes are shut. I yawn. Babies have no real idea of occasion.

"What are you calling her?" someone asks the question, a voice, filled with compassion for this sorry scene, belonging to one of the nurses. My mother gathers me close again and stares at my face which by now, may well have lost its squashed nosed, red cheeked appearance. Maybe I am a beauty after all.

"We haven't decided for sure. We did think we might call a girl, Joy," perhaps too much hope will be pinned to that name? "but looking at her, I don't think so," Well, no need to discount it out of hand is there?

"I will wait until he wakes up," my mother decides. I suppose I must resign myself to being baby Robinson for a little longer.

I am sucking on a rubber teat. My mother could not cope with me savaging her breasts it seems and with the shock of the accident and my father's apparent vegetable state, her milk has dried up. A nurse is feeding me. My mother is with George.

I meet my brother a few hours later. Gran is visiting and she picks me up and cuddles me and makes a big fuss of my tiny self. She even wants to give me a bottle. She refers to my mother as, Becky.

"Becky, won't you hold her for a little while?"

"I have been holding her," snaps Becky, "I just need to be with George, George needs me more."

She sweeps out of the room and I am cradled in Gran's lap until my brother climbs up onto the chair to see.

"Meet Joe," says Gran. I like Joe. He has a round, freckled face and jet black hair. Maybe I will have jet black hair. Joe touches my face and I feel his soft skin against mine as he cuddles me. He smells of what I will come to know as marmite. I will always love marmite. Gran hugs us both and I think she is crying.

"Everything will be fine little ones, don't you fret," she is fumbling in her handbag and pulling something out, "and this is your Granddad,"

I see a pair of bright blue eyes, shaded by enormous black, bushy brows, peering down at me from within a photo frame. The eyes smile.

"He would have adored you," Gran whispers.

Of course, none of this means much to me at the time. From what I gather as I grow older, George had no living parents when I was born. Granddad Rob, might have been a good ally, had he not smoked himself into an early grave.

It is a strange set of circumstances that greet my arrival in this world. Not that I am aware of this at the time of course. All these things are told to me later and wedge themselves into my memory like blocks of play dough, moulded to fit and bound never to look the same again.

Joe nuzzles my hair, what little I have of it, and begins singing a lullaby. Gran joins in. We present a pretty tableau to anyone walking by the ward that night.

Becky returns when I am asleep in my plastic sided box. I sense she is there but I prefer not to wake. Maybe she strokes my cheek, maybe she checks my fingers and toes. I will never know. When I wake, she has gone again – George's need is greater than mine. I am more than thirty-six hours old.

It is almost Christmas. I sleep in a wicker crib by Becky's bed. George has woken up. He can speak, just a little. He can recognise people.

"Thank the Lord," says Gran.

There is hope. I have a name, Hannah Joy. Hannah for grace or favour, according to Becky's book of baby names and Joy, for the joy I bring. I am not sure what joy I give Becky. I feel I am a rather annoying encumbrance most of the time.

"This child has the gift, I'll be bound," says Gran when she catches me staring into space with a frown furrowing my baby brow. Granddad just smiles at me from a photograph on the wall. His eyes speak volumes.

"She looks as though she has the answer to everything," Gran finishes. I would like to say that I don't. Most of the time, I am staring and trying to focus on a scratch on the window or a mark on the wall. Becky just shrugs and packs another thermos into her bag, throwing me an air kiss before she leaves.

Christmas comes and goes, periods of festive laughter punctuated by the sound of Becky's retreating footsteps as she trudges to the car and heads off to the hospital.

I have been residing in the family home for several weeks. I am accustomed to Gran and am happy to seek her out for my every need. Glimpses of Becky are rare. Becky almost lives at the hospital. Most of the time, we are three, Gran, Joe and me. We drop Joe at pre-school and Gran fusses over me. By the time Becky comes home, tears dried on her cheeks, lipstick applied in a half-hearted attempt at normality, mascara running, I am settled for the night and barely notice her as she creeps in to give me a goodnight kiss. She will regret this one day but for now, she doesn't have a choice.

By Easter, I have grown chubby and can sit up on my own. I am almost crawling. Joe helps me by dragging me along by my arms until Gran intervenes. I am more than content to sit and watch. I watch Joe line up his cars and pretend to be a plane as he runs around and around the coffee table with his arms held wide. I laugh; I make explosive noises. My hair is growing. It is mouse brown, almost red in some lights, not dark like Joe's but I don't mind.

As summer arrives, I am crawling along the floor and getting into everything. Becky is spending more time at home, preparing. She is painting the dining room and I sit in my walker, watching as she applies apple-white to the walls. The room has a big bed in it, high, like the hospital beds. There is equipment for lifting and two sticks lean up against the far wall. George is coming home.

I am nine months old when George is wheeled through the doors. He has to be brought in through the French windows because no ordinary door is wide enough for the chair. The dining room has been turned into a bedroom for him. I recognise him because I have been visiting him since I was just an hour old, but George is a stranger. I think he is a stranger to Gran and to Joe too. Or, perhaps, it is more accurate to say, they are strangers to him. He doesn't speak much, he just stares and frowns at everything. His head is no longer bandaged but he has a livid scar across his temple. I see a little more of Becky because she no longer has to go to the hospital every day but responsibility for my day to day care, still lies with Gran. Becky's attention is still fixed on George.

September, George is walking with one stick and he is speaking, almost as before but for a slight stammer. The hospital bed and the wheel chair have gone and he is ensconced in the marital bed, upstairs once more. To all outward appearances, he is normal.

"Thank the Lord," sighs Gran.

George's moods are far from normal. He is subject to violent outbursts followed by tearful apology. There are times when even Becky runs out of the room in tears, unable to cope any longer. There is a period of turmoil in the house from which I hide until Gran scoops me out from beneath the table or from behind the curtain and comforts me as the voices rage. This state of affairs, seems set to continue throughout my formative years.

I am three today, the same age as Joe was, when I was born. Today, George has a pivotal Consultant's appointment. He has made good progress, all things considered. He has gone back to work – an office based job, for three days a week and his mood swings have grown less frequent. He has a tremor in his right hand and he tires easily but the doctors are pleased with his progress. However, he is unlikely to make a complete recovery. This, watered down version of George, is the best we can hope for. Everyone looks very serious when they hear this news. Even Gran fails to say anything to lighten the mood. I snuggle into Gran's jumper and play with her beads. One day I will recognise the seriousness of this moment for what it is. Right now, I am the only one who has never known George to be any other way.

From this day, my third birthday, life becomes more settled. I begin to get to know Becky a little better than before and find I quite like her on a good day, when she isn't under the influence of her medication. I am not sure what the medication is but she says the tablets stop her going crazy. Looking after my father for three years has taken its toll and continues to challenge her. She sleeps more while on the medication and is less anxious.

We settle into a routine. George leaves for work at 7am, three days a week. It is winter so is still dark when he reverses the car out of the drive. The headlights illuminate my bedroom and tell me it is time to get up. Joe helps me get my breakfast. Joe helps me get dressed and when Gran arrives at 8.30am, I am ready to be taken to pre-school. As a rule, Becky emerges from the bedroom just before we leave the house. She gives me a hug and tells me to be good. Gran tells her to take it easy and chivvies us into her car. Becky waves at us from the kitchen window.

"Wave at your Mum," Gran says, so I do. Joe raises one hand but doesn't bother to look.

At night, I sit on George's lap after dinner and he tells me stories from when he was a little boy. Joe sometimes listens too. George makes us laugh and I think he is quite a good sort after all. I don't recall Becky telling me stories, it is not something that she tends to do. The stories George tells, can be funny but we know we can't expect them to last long. After a while, he becomes irritable and shoos us away. The in between times are good though.

When I am five years old, George takes me to choose a Christmas tree. I am sitting in the front seat of his sky-blue Citroën. The seat belt is tight round my middle. I fidget and he shouts, just a little and then remembers to apologise. I am used to it. I force myself to sit very still.

It is cold in the field where the trees are stacked, and a thin layer of snow carpets the floor. George is trying to be calm and patient as I wander amongst the piles of trees, looking for that one, that perfect one. He is already regretting telling me I can choose it.

"Oh, hurry up Hannah, for goodness sake…" I hear the impatience in his voice. I detect the effort it has taken him not to raise it. I try to be quick but there are so many trees. "What about this one, dear?"

The lady in front of me is wearing an oversized red jumper and a white woolly hat. She is of course wearing other things but the jumper and the hat are what stand out to me. I stare at her. She is pulling up a tallish bundle and shaking it out. It looks like a Christmas tree now I suppose.

"Yes, yes, that one will do," George calls in relief. He marches over, only a slight limp impeding his progress across the icy ground, and takes the trunk from the woman in red.

"How much?" he asks.
The woman smiles. I am taken aback by her smile. It is dazzling. She laughs and shakes her head,

"Oh, I don't work here but I know how hard it is to choose a tree and your daughter was having trouble," George thanks her and drags the tree to the kiosk where a short, wiry man, is counting out pennies.

I thank the woman too. She watches us cross the car park and I have a strange feeling she knows me. She doesn't choose a tree herself, she gets into her car and sits there, watching us. I tell George. George glances across and tells me not to be silly. She must be waiting for someone. The tree won't fit in the car. It has to be tied to the roof rack. All the while, the woman watches.

I climb into my seat and George revs the engine. I can't see the woman in the car any longer because there are so many trees in the way but I bet she is still there, watching. I can't get her smile out of my head, a dazzling, yet almost manic smile.

Becky says that the tree will do even if the journey home has divested it of half its needles. "Must have happened when we went under that low bridge," George is smiling. He smiles more and more these days which is sort of nice. That must be an improvement, mustn't it? Maybe the doctors are wrong. He walks with that limp and he still has dreadful moods but they are experimenting with new drugs. The new drugs make him happy, he says.
I wish Becky would find some new drugs.

I spend a lot of time reading. I can lose myself in a good book. I find sanctuary there. Joe calls me a bookworm. He spends a lot of time with George, "making up for lost time," they call it. Maybe that's what I am doing with Becky when she is not under the influence of those pills. We sit and read our books together, side by side, not touching, not communicating, just being. I am not sure she is reading at all. I watch her sometimes, the way her eyes flick across the page, unseeing, the way she licks her lips and sighs. After a while, I grow bored with watching and read my book.

The years go by. George improves a little but never quite gets back to the way he was before his accident. Not that I know how that was. Becky continues taking her pills but she acts more like my idea of a normal mother. We go shopping and then we can giggle and laugh together. Sometimes, she manages to get through an entire day without slipping into her zombie-like state. At others, the pills seem to take her away from me for weeks at a time. My insides twist during those weeks. Still, as the months and years go by, we are doing ok.

"Thank the Lord," says Gran.

We are doing ok even when we hear we will have to move many miles away from Gran and she can no longer be there at the drop of a hat. George has been offered a better job now. He works five days a week at the new company and, despite the Doctor's gloomy predictions, seems to be improving. We can afford a bigger house. Things should be looking up.

Joe and I change schools. I make new friends but I quite liked living where we lived before and I miss Gran. Now, when Becky aims a vacant stare into space and disappears to her room to lie down, I don't have Gran to turn to. The twisted feelings inside me, get worse. I imagine my insides are now tied up like the ends of a balloon, pulled into impossible knots that won't undo. I wish I could float away like a balloon.

I don't think Becky likes the new house very much. She and George argue a lot. I haven't known them argue quite so much as this before. George accuses her of being reliant on tablets. That's rich, considering he pops at least ten a day himself in the name of "recovery". Joe and I learn when to stay clear of them both. We are relieved when

Gran decides to visit and stays for a few days. A tenuous peace settles on the house while she is here. I hear her and Becky talking late at night. It seems everyone knows what is going on except me. George and Becky might separate, that's what I hear, as the moon slips behind a cloud. No one says anything to me, even though they must know I have overheard them. I wait, my stomach twisting in fresh knots every time I hear them raise their voices. They don't separate. They just continue to bicker and get on one another's nerves.

It is getting near Christmas again. My twelfth birthday comes and goes. Becky bemoans the fact that we are living in town and George admits he misses the Devon countryside where we used to live. Gran has popped over for the afternoon. Becky asks her if the cottage would be available for Christmas. I don't know which cottage this is. No one enlightens me. Gran says she will ask. I don't know who she will ask. I don't bother to enquire. I plug in my earphones and listen to Dizzee Rascal, rather than to their voices.

December 2012

The car is bumping over the snow covered ruts in the road, sliding across patches of hardened ice and gliding towards the moon. I am scrunched up in a ball in the corner, my seat belt not worth its salt right now but I don't care. If we come to a staggering stop, I might well be strangled by the thing.

"Sit up Hannah,"

That's Becky's voice, dull and not quite of this world. How many tablets has she taken already today? I picture them on her bedside table. She lays them out in a line and eats them up, one by one, two pink, one yellow, three blue and two white capsules that calm her nerves.

Once she has eaten these, she moves on to my father's side. He will be sleeping of course. He sleeps a lot. She spreads his daily drugs out on a raffia mat on which he keeps his water glass on the bedside table.

He has more tablets than her. His are arranged in lines of green and blue. There are two powders in sachets and there is a pot of cream which he rubs into his muscles every evening. The new job tires him but he won't admit it. He says he can cope but he is short tempered and irritable most of the time now.

It seems the cottage was vacant when Gran enquired, because Becky announced that we are all going down to Devon for Christmas to stay in it. I am only going without putting up a fight because Gran will be there too. Gran is squashed into the back seat between us at the moment, with Joe who is playing on his Smartphone and oblivious to the world on one side and me, curled up in the corner. I am also curious to know what a cottage called, Angel Cottage, will be like.

"Hannah," repeats Becky.

"She's ok," says Gran and smiles at me, patting my leg.

All I know about this trip is that we are going to Devon to stay in a cottage where we will all have a brilliant time. It will be therapeutic, Gran tells us. Becky and George deserve the break. Joe grunts and I smile. Joe is fifteen and sullen, I am twelve and "a little madam" according to Becky.

"But perfectly normal, thank the Lord," Gran always interjects.

They put my nightmares down to George's accident. I have seen psychiatrists and therapists and they all put my sometimes weird behaviour, down to Post Traumatic Stress. Becky is less sure.

"She was born after the accident for God's sake!" she protests, when Ms Colleridge, my current therapist, tells her.

"It affected her for years," reminds Gran, "Children absorb things,"

Becky watches me with extra care from then on. This holiday is supposed to help us bond. A bit late for that, if you ask me but I will go along with it. It will be made bearable because Gran is here.

George is driving. Becky prefers to do the driving if she can but George likes to be in control. Becky clutches the seat whenever we turn a corner.

"You are going too fast – slow down – watch the kerb," she keeps up a constant tirade of commands. I think George ought to tell her to keep quiet but he doesn't. He ignores her for the most part. I sometimes think Becky and George will end up getting divorced. I have friends at school whose parents have split up. It doesn't seem so bad. I voiced the notion to Joe a while ago but he just pooh-poohed it.

Sometimes, I think they still love each other but at others, like now for instance, I think they can't stand to be near one other. As though to prove me wrong, George reaches out and pats Becky's knee. I can see it in the driver's mirror. Becky smiles and for a moment I think I might be wrong. Then the car swerves to the left, Becky screams at George and George's face closes.

"Black ice," he murmurs and we all make a sound like the air being sucked from a vacuum.

The drive is long and tedious. I have eaten the snacks I packed, read the book I stowed in my backpack — well, reading made me feel sick so I had to stop—and Joe and I are now playing a babyish game of I Spy. George's face loses its tightness and he joins in. Becky joins in too and I can see that pleases Gran. After half an hour in which Joe and I try to outdo one another with fcis —fence covered in snow and tcws — tree covered with snow, we call it quits and resume our silent progress. The game has softened the atmosphere though. George and Becky begin chatting in an amicable tone.

The car is forging its way through the drifts that rise up either side. The windscreen wipers struggle to keep pace with the flakes that cover it. The car windscreen heater is turned to maximum but the ice does not melt on contact.

Every few yards, George gets out to knock more snow away so he can see. We all shiver as the icy wind sneaks in and whips around the car but we'd all rather be inside than out. George has to fiddle with the car door to get it to shut. He swears beneath his breath. I wait for Becky to tell him off but she doesn't. Has she taken another tablet?

I slump back down in my seat and count the ruts in the road as we go over them. I think of George in his car that night, when it swerved off the road and landed in a ditch. It was snowing then.

I had to talk about the accident with the psychiatrist and bring up all those memories that I had buried. I still have the nightmares. The woman from the car park with the Christmas tree hovers on the perimeter of them, watching, her face wreathed in a manic smile. My dreams are peopled with shadows but her smile is always there, clear and sharp and disturbing.

Of late, the nightmares have become more frequent. Becky says it is my age, George doesn't say an awful lot but he winks at me. George and I have bonded well over the years to my surprise.

Joe and I are still close, despite the sullen teenage moods and the big brother versus kid sister thing. Joe says coming away will just be an excuse for more bickering between our parents. It's hard to decide if they still love each other sometimes or whether they just tolerate each other because one thing is for sure, we don't witness much affection between them.

Gran says they are stressed. She says that love takes many forms and sometimes people don't express it very well but they feel it, deep inside. She thumps her chest when she says this.

I wonder if Becky is feeling that love when she screams at George because he has taken a wrong turning. She is holding her forehead because she has 'one of her heads' coming on. Gran tells her to calm down and Joe sniggers into his phone. I hunker down a bit further into the leather.

Becky hasn't told us much about the cottage in Devon except that it is a miracle it is available at such short notice at Christmas. She says it belongs to someone Gran knows. I suppose that's how we got it. Gran hasn't mentioned the cottage before as far as I know, though she must have mentioned it to Becky I suppose. All I know is that Gran checked it out and found that it was available. She booked it for us at once. I thought she seemed very excited by the idea at the time. I know she worries about Becky and George. Maybe this trip will help.

"Angel Cottage," Becky mused, ignoring Joe's derisory snort.

"I think it sounds perfect," I told her.

"It's a long drive," Becky kept saying. George just shrugged. He does that a lot. It irks Becky that he won't take any responsibility for decisions. It just seems to irritate her. I sometimes wonder what it was like before the accident. Joe doesn't remember much. Gran just says we were a very happy family. I sometimes think it was my being born that changed things. Was I just one thing too much to cope with? I tell no one this, except the psychiatrist of course.

When the accident features in my nightmares, I see a tangled mass of metal in a ditch and lots of blood. I have to imagine it because, after all, I was not there to see it. Sometimes, imagining is worse than seeing. I don't see my father but I know he is there somewhere, buried in the wreckage. The psychiatrist tells me this is my way of coping with something else that is worrying me. It is impossible for me to know what happened that night but by creating a false memory, I am forcing myself to feel a guilt for what happened while suppressing the real memory that I need to deal with. I am suppressing a host of guilty feelings according to her. These feelings of guilt come out in my subconscious when I am asleep. She tells me that the woman whose smile I see, has entered my sub conscious because I was traumatised by the experience of buying the Christmas tree. I told her once that my father had shouted at me that day, when I fidgeted too much. I don't remember feeling traumatised. I don't think I will tell her much more. Maybe I will just keep quiet about anything else that happens.

I sit up in the car now and stare out of the window. The world beyond the car is white. Snow falls, thick and fast. Overhead tree branches, weighed down with the stuff, scrape on the roof. The heater continues to blast out heat but makes little impact. I wonder if we could die out here in this white, wilderness? The Devon lanes all look the same and George is having difficulty navigating their twists and turns. A fallen tree impedes our progress and George swears, Becky tells him off and Joe sniggers. I ignore them all. We manage to turn the car around. We'll have to find another route through.
Gran pats my knee.

"Can't see a damned thing," George mutters after a while.

I wonder if this journey is reminding him of the accident. Do his memories of it match my own? I check myself, of course, my memories are not real, they can't be.

I dare not ask him if he remembers. I imagine what it would be like to be stuck in a ditch, a twisted metal box on top of you, unable to call for help, cold…alone…Gran nudges me and the horrific thoughts are stopped. I follow her gaze. A lone stag is standing on the embankment, watching us.

"Rudolph!" I laugh.

Joe looks too. The stag stands there, watching us edge along the track for several minutes before it ambles off into the woods. I am filled with hope though I don't know why. Half an hour later and George has stopped the car and is staring at the map, spread out before him. The SatNav has given up the ghost.

"This can't be the way, he is saying, shaking his head,

"There's nothing down here,"

"It must be," Becky has taken the map and is running her finger along the crease, "Let's go on a bit further and see if we can find someone to ask.

We all groan. We haven't seen anyone thus far and we've been driving for hours down these winding lanes. Gran should know the way. She lives a mere thirty miles from here but she hasn't been here for a very long time, not since Becky was a child, she apologises.

"In the snow, all the lanes look alike."

"Anyone have a signal?" George knows it is a dim hope, Becky and he have been trying to use their mobiles to call the owner every few miles. Becky holds her mobile up to the roof and wiggles it round for a bit,

"No,"

"Nor me," Gran says, doing the same.

Joe is peering through the glass.

"There's a sign," he says, pointing. We all look. George gets out. The tip of a road sign is just visible under a mound of snow. George brushes the snow off and reads it out,

"Next left!" he shouts with excitement creeping into his voice, "Well done, Joe,"

I am pleased for Joe. Joe has suffered more than me over the past few years and he never seems to do much right in George's eyes of late.

"Good one," says Becky and reaches round to pat his knee. Joe flinches but I know he is pleased even if he won't show it.

We take the next left and the track narrows, if that is possible.

"This doesn't even look like a road," says Becky.

"I remember it is pretty remote…" Gran murmurs.

"Well, the sign says Angel Cottage is this way," George is determined now. He pushes ahead, almost cheery when getting out to push the snow off the windscreen every few yards.

Then we see it.

Out of nowhere, it appears. A small, tumble down cottage in the middle of a field of white. Lamplight shines through the window, pooling on the snow, making it sparkle like magic. The drive and the path to the front door have been cleared, a recent activity by the looks of things. A small barn is tucked in next to the cottage in a snow covered courtyard and we park our car here.

"Is there a key?" Becky voices the obvious question.

"It is supposed to be under a flowerpot," Gran says, hesitating. Everything in the yard appears to be buried by the snow. If there has been a flower pot here, it will be under that blanket somewhere by now.

"It's open," George grins, pushing the back door wide so that we can all troop across the threshold.

The kitchen has a log burner which is lit and throws out heat as we enter. The welcome warmth draws us all in. Two rosy cheeked cherubs gaze down at us from the wall. More of the same adorn the cupboards and shelves.

I look around, expecting to see the owner waiting to greet us.

She or he, has gone it seems, perhaps they got tired of waiting. We are very late. Our route must have taken us miles out of the way. A note is propped up on the kitchen table next to the key. Becky picks up the note and reads with a smile.

"She says, she has left everything ready for us and hopes we have a wonderful Christmas. We are to feel free to explore the house and the barn. She says she will call in at some point as she is only in the village."

I wonder which village the woman is referring to as we did not pass one but that is mere detail now that we are here.

George is looking almost happy as he settles himself by the fire with a mug of tea and Becky has unpacked and made the place feel like home by putting a few of our personal things around the room and stowing the presents beneath the tree, which the owner has put in the living room. It is a real tree, decorated with coloured lights and tinsel.

"It's like something from the sixties," Becky laughs but in secret, I think she loves it. I am fascinated by the strands of silver lametta that hang from the branches like icicles. They twist and turn beneath the lights. There is a star sitting on the topmost branch. That is disappointing for some reason. I had expected an angel this being Angel Cottage. The star is beautiful. Perhaps there are already enough Angels about the place.

I want to explore outside but it is late and very dark. Becky and George are watching a film on the television. I ask Joe if he wants to come with me but he grunts something about doing it tomorrow and goes back to his game.

I wander into the kitchen. I am struck by the number of plaster angels on show here. I have a feeling these are permanent residents and are not just brought out for Christmas. Cherubs adorn the back door and a clock on the wall depicts a bevy of winged beings smiling down on us all. Not to everybody's taste I am sure, but it fits well enough. The kitchen is modern but what Becky calls, 'retro'. I am about to open the back door when Gran appears.

"Hey, what are you up to?" she asks in that way she has. I draw back and grin,

"I was just going to look outside," I tell her.

"Well, let's sneak out together eh?" she winks at me. Side by side, we push the back door open. A rush of cold air almost knocks us off our feet and we pull it to again with a gasp.

"This requires a coat and boots," decides Gran and I am pleased because she is going to come with me. I can always count on Gran. We grab the coats that have been hung on hooks next to the door and slip our feet into the wellies that Becky has placed beneath. You have to give Becky her due, she thinks of everything.

"Ready?"

I am. Gran pushes the door open again and this time holds on to it so that it doesn't drag us out before we are ready.

Pushing the door closed behind us, I thrust my hands deep in my pockets. Gran links her arm through mine, I am almost as tall as her these days, or maybe she is shrinking. It is hard to tell. We trudge through the snow towards the barn, the wind biting at our chins and noses.

A slither of a moon has come out and lights a path. I can't help but feel there is magic in the air as we grow closer to the great barn door. Gran lifts the latch and tugs it open. We step inside.

It is not much warmer in here than outside but at least the wind has gone.

Gran thinks to look for a light switch and the barn is all at once flooded with a dim yellow glow. It is clear that this place has not been used for anything but storage for a while. Boxes are piled up on one side, along with an old bike and several broken chairs. There is a ladder straight ahead. I am climbing it before Gran can object. She stands at the bottom watching my progress with a worried frown. I feel the rough wood splintering beneath my skin, and the smell of old straw and mildew fills the air. Gloves would be helpful – mine are back at the cottage. I get to the top with ease.

I am standing on the loft floor, Gran looking up at me, when I see the girl. At least, I think I see the girl. She is about my age I'd say, wearing a pale blue pinafore and has her hair tied into a pony tail. She is staring at me. I gasp and Gran calls up,

"What's the matter? I think you had better come down, Hannah, I don't want to have to climb up after you,"

At the sound of her voice, it seems the girl vanishes so that I am no longer certain she was ever there at all. I stare at the spot she was occupying only a moment before, then find myself clambering back down the splintered rungs.

I want to tell Gran about the girl but she will think I am imagining things, I am sure. Maybe I was. I look back but there is no one there now. It must have been a trick of the light.

"It's a bit spooky up there," I admit and Gran laughs.

"Well, maybe we will come back when it is daylight. Easy to feel a bit spooked in this light," she shivers, "let's go back to the house,"

I am happy to follow. I am not sure what it is that I saw but there is something here, I know it. Of course, I tell myself, I have a vivid imagination, I may have just dreamt the girl up.

By the time we have crossed the courtyard to the house, I am almost convinced I imagined it. There are rags and boxes in the loft, a shaft of light must have played tricks with my eyes. Yet, in truth, I am not sure of it at all.
"Been exploring?" Becky is laughing at us. We must look a little bedraggled and our noses are red from the cold,

"Mum, you should know better!" but the rebuke is softened by Becky's newly acquired calm and she doesn't say much more. Gran squeezes my hand and we grin at each other like the conspirators we are.
Joe looks up as I plonk myself down on the sofa next to him.

"What's up, Twig?"

I hate it when he calls me that baby name at home but I don't even notice today.

"The barn was a bit…spooky," I tell him with a shrug.

"Spooky eh? Seeing ghosts?" he teases.
I laugh, unwilling to confide in him, my suspicions could yet be unfounded.

"Just spooky," I repeat.

I am almost asleep when I hear someone creep into my room. Soft footsteps tread by my bed. I almost expect to see the girl from the barn but no, it is Gran.

"Are you awake, Hannah?"
The question is rhetorical, I have already sat up and am rubbing the remains of sleep from my eyes.

"What do you want?"

Gran sits on the end of my bed her weight making the mattress sag a little more. She is wearing her rose pink dressing gown and a pair of oversized, fluffy pink slippers. A pink blancmange comes to mind. I suppress a giggle and wait.

"I've been thinking,"

"Yes?" I wait.

"Well, I know you have not had it easy, with your nightmares and...well, if you think this place makes it worse, we can always go home,"

I stare at her in surprise. What an odd thing to say.

"I just want you to know that I am here for you Hannah, for always," she finishes.

I am touched. I doubt this place will make my nightmares worse. As a matter of fact, I am already feeling far calmer and a lot more settled than I have for a long time. I want to tell her this but the words sound strange even to my ears. Instead, I smile and shake my head,

"No Gran, I love it here, really. I just got a bit spooked in the barn, that's all, it was silly,"

"Well, if you are sure, you get a good night's sleep then."

I get the feeling she wants to say more but though I wait, she just smiles.

She leans forward, dropping a kiss on my brow before going back to her own room. I stare after her retreating figure. I am puzzled. She seems to have over reacted to my earlier outburst in the barn, I think. Does she know something that I don't? I know she knows the owner of this place. Maybe it is haunted! Who is afraid of ghosts? Not me. I lie back down and pull the covers up to my chin. I can't put my finger on it but something begs me to keep this quiet, this vision of a girl, a ghost, or whatever it is. I smile to myself and close my eyes but sleep will not come at first. I lie here staring at the ceiling and thinking about the barn for some time before sleep claims me at last.

It's another white day as far as I can tell, lying here, watching the dawn break through the gap in the curtain. A long silver finger of light reaches to the wardrobe. I stare at it for a while, the grain of the wood in sharp relief where the light touches it.

The cottage is stretching back to life. I lie here listening to it creak and yawn as it wakes from a night's slumber. A wintery sun forces itself to make an appearance and a robin lands on the windowsill. I can see him through the gap, black beady eyes darting around. If I had a few crumbs, I'd put them out for him.

I can hear noises echoing up from downstairs, the sound of crockery chinking, cutlery being set on the table. Becky or Gran. Whoever it is, they are up early.

"Still snowing," George says, as he emerges from the bathroom, drying his hair with a towel. I nod. He shuffles off to the bedroom to dress. He tends to get faster as the day goes on. In the morning, he shuffles.

I am downstairs in a few moments, dressed and ready to go exploring in daylight. I intend going back into the barn to see if I notice anything else. Gran need not worry. I am not about to give myself nightmares. It is with some surprise that I realise that I did not dream at all last night so there were no nightmares.

"Have you seen the snug yet?" Gran is excited because she has another room to show me that I didn't see last night. It is tucked in between the dining room and the kitchen. Three steps down and we are in the snug. I have to agree it is very cosy. An open fire, left ready to light by the looks of it, has been laid in the grate and there is a beautiful, squashy sofa just like the one in Gran's house. I curl up in it, experimenting for a later read. It is more than comfortable. I almost melt into its leathery folds.

"I knew you'd like it and look, there are lots of books and games over here, I remember coming here as a child and playing with some of these," Gran has opened a cupboard to reveal a pile of old games, Ludo, Cluedo,

Drafts and Monopoly. The books appeal to me more. I will look at them in detail later.

Joe pokes his head around the door frame and raises an eyebrow.

"Hey, sic!" he comments.

"I take it that's good?" Gran teases, shaking her head. He ignores her and ambles back to the kitchen, "Porridge is up," he manages, before he leaves.

We eat in the kitchen at the old pine table that looks as though it has borne the imprint of many a child's pen over the years. It is now half covered by a gingham cloth and a sprig of holly sits in a jar in the centre. The clock on the wall ticks away the minutes, the cherubs beaming down at us as we tuck into our porridge.

"I don't like that clock," Becky remarks, gives me the creeps, those eyes follow you round the room."

"Oh, I don't know Becky, there is something rather sweet about it," Gran says, between mouthfuls.

"It's not keeping time very well," Joe grunts and I say nothing. My head is too full of the apparition I believe I saw last night.

It is almost ten o'clock by the time I am free to go back to the barn.

"Be careful in there!" Becky calls.

"I will."

I am half way across the courtyard when I stop. What is that I can hear? A dog barking? I look around the garden. Then I see him. A small brown and white dog "of dubious parentage" Gran would say. He is standing by the barn door and barking at me.

"Hey, it's ok boy," I say, holding out my hand. He growls and takes a step back. Is he afraid of me? I bend down and make soothing noises. The little dog edges forward and lets me pat him. His fur is soft and silky, his tail begins to wag and he licks my hand with a rough, warm pink tongue. I kneel down and check his collar. There is a tag on which I read, "Buster,"

"Well, hello Buster, where have you come from?" I ask as I fuss him.

Buster licks me some more giving my face a good clean.

I stand up and take a look around. The gate is shut so he must have come through the hedge. Maybe there are more houses here than we saw last night. I am considering taking a walk up the lane, just to see, when I turn back to find the little dog has vanished.

I spend a short time looking in the hedgerow to see if I can see a hole but he is so small I dare say he could squeeze through any gap. I whistle but he doesn't appear. Oh well, he looked well fed, not a stray and there was his collar…

I push all thoughts of the little dog from my mind and turn my attention to the barn door. The snow has drifted against the door overnight and I have to scrape it away with my hands, before it will budge. Again, I wish I had worn gloves. By the time I am through, my hands are red and raw. I would like to ask Joe to help but part of me wants to explore on my own. Despite it being daylight, the barn is quite dark inside. I flick the switch and wait as the pale light floods the floor.

There are things I missed seeing last night. Last night I went straight to the ladder. Now, I take a walk around the ground floor of the barn. I note the piles of kindling, I presume they were left for the stove and the fire, the sacks of straw and the gardening tools arranged in a neat line on the far wall. There is a box containing garden toys, including a bat and ball. They all look pretty old. I guess they belong to the owner who would have had them as a child. Becky has a couple of books and a doll from her childhood. I am not allowed to touch them. It appears the owner of these old things, would like us to use them. I pick up the bat and ball and bounce the ball a few times on the hard floor. I think I hear the little dog bark again but when I peer out into the garden, he is not there. He must be on the other side of the hedge now.

Back in the barn, I sift through the toys for a bit before I make my way to the ladder. It looks different in daylight. A shaft of sunlight has reached the upper floor so the light is not needed up there. I don't turn it off.

A trickle of fear runs down my spine as I put my foot on the first rung. Will she be there? Was she just a figment of my imagination? I take the first few steps slowly, gripping the sides with my frozen fingers. I find it hard to look up. I keep my eyes on the rungs until I am at last at the top. This time, I step onto the boards with care and look around.

There is something different from last night. I am trying to think what it is when I realise, a window has swung open and a blast of icy air is blowing through the gap. The smell of mildewed straw has gone. I cross to the window and pull it closed. Peering out, I can see right across the garden to the fields beyond. The entire landscape is covered in white. A church spire gleams in the distance, the village maybe? There are no buildings close to the cottage that I can see, not in this direction anyway. Perhaps the little dog walked up from the village? Maybe it isn't so far away after all.

Something moves in the garden below. I expect to see the dog again but it isn't the dog. My heart thuds in my chest. I can't be sure but it looks, it looks as though it is a girl, the girl from last night perhaps, running into the cottage. I blink but the image vanishes. Am I just imagining things now? I suspect that wanting to see something so much is making me believe I have seen it. Drawing back from the window, I survey the loft. The trunk sits square in the corner. An old coat hangs on a hook above it. Could I have imagined that to be a person? I don't think so. The girl from last night was standing in the shadows but she was a girl, not an old coat.

"You have such a vivid imagination!" I imagine Gran saying if I were to tell her, "I just went outside to put the rubbish in the bin, I bet it was me you saw, silly girl." Perhaps I am being unfair, Gran is known to be open minded about most things. Am I seeing things now as well as having nightmares though? Are the nightmares being replaced with daytime terrors? I wonder what the psychiatrist would say about that. I decide I won't be telling her. I turn off the light and close the door, half hoping the little dog will be waiting outside. I could do with his warm furry little body to cuddle and the rasp of his tongue on my cheek. He is not there.

Becky is rolling out pastry on the kitchen table. This is a surprise in itself, since I have not known her to be that keen on baking before. She is more the sort of person who will defrost something from the supermarket rather than make it from scratch. Is this place having an effect on her too? It seems so, because she is looking very relaxed with no trace of having taken any of the tablets that turn her into a zombie. There is something in the way she wields the rolling pin that makes me smile. I watch as she pushes it to and fro across the dough. I realise I am staring.

"Sausage rolls," she explains as though pre-empting any smart comment that might come from my lips, adding,

"Did you have any nightmares last night?"
I am surprised to find that for the first time in ages, I am able to say I did not dream last night.
There you are then, it's working already," Becky retorts in triumph.

"What is?"

"This place, getting away from it all. I feel this cottage has a healing element to it. Don't you feel it Mum?"

"Well, it's peaceful I must say," Gran agrees, with unusual reticence as she pokes some more wood into the stove,

"Yes, peaceful, as though nothing bad has ever happened here. I noticed the tranquillity as soon as we stepped inside. It has the gentle atmosphere of a happy home. Good for the soul."

Since Becky is not prone to such profound comments as a rule, we all look at her in surprise.

"What?" she laughs and goes back to rolling the pastry.

"We'll need more wood soon," Gran comments.

"I know where there's some wood," I say.

"In the barn, according to the information here," George waves an information manual in our direction, "I'll go get some."

"I saw a dog out there earlier," I tell them, remembering Buster who has been pushed from my mind until now by the ghost girl, whose presence I am now beginning to doubt again.

"A dog?"

"Yes, a pretty little dog, he was ever so cute but he vanished, through the hedge. He had a tag on his collar, he's called Buster."

"I expect he lives on the farm over the way or comes up from the village," guesses Gran, adding with a smile, "I used to know a little dog called Buster, must be a common name," before standing up and brushing her hands on her Jeans to rid them of smuts.

I suppose she is right. I might go out and see if he is still out there after dinner. I wouldn't like to think of him being lost and cold.

I turn to hang my coat on its peg. As I reach for the hook, I give an involuntary shiver. The hairs on the back of my neck are standing on end and the atmosphere in the kitchen has changed. I spin back to face the room in time to see everything brought into sharp focus, the colours over bright, objects larger than life. Am I having some sort of seizure? As I watch, the room returns to normal, colours and objects settling with an almost imperceptible calm. My mouth is dry. I swallow hard and blink. Everything seems to have rolled back into place. I look around and check but it seems that no one else has noticed anything untoward. The hands on the Angel clock judder and Becky nods at it, with a frown,

"See? It's running fast again."
What is happening to me? I don't have time to wonder for long.

George returns from the barn with his bundle of wood, which he tips into the scuttle by the stove. The simple action is somehow pleasing to watch. When have I seen him do such a thing before? Never. He is acting like— what? A normal father, that's it, he is acting like a normal father. Becky is right about this place; it is doing us all good.

I am sitting in the snug, on the squashy leather sofa. Despite the roaring fire, which Gran lit earlier, the air is still chilled in here. I pull on my Fleece, a birthday present from Becky and George, with the five Olympic rings on its chest, and curl my feet beneath me. The card I have written to them, now stands on the mantelpiece. It sparkles in the firelight. I am pleased with the one I chose, the glittering snow scene, with its thatched cottage and rolling white fields, looks, for all the world, like this very place. I couldn't have known of course. I bought the card before ever setting eyes on Angel Cottage.

A copy of Dickens's, A Christmas Carol, lies unopened on my lap. Perhaps I will read it later, in bed. The fire crackles in the grate, the flames casting eerie shadows on the walls as they flicker and burn. Tomorrow will be Christmas Eve. I want to savour every moment. I love

Christmas. This is of course thanks to Gran. She has always taken great pains to make it magical for us children and even now we are older, she does not let us forget that this is a very special time for us. To be fair, she has had to work hard to keep it that way over the years. Becky and George always approach Christmas with a form of dread. It reminds them of the worst time of their lives perhaps. Why this year should be different, I do not know but I sense the difference in their every move. Becky has made several rounds of sausage rolls and mince pies, she has added her own marzipan decorations to the tree, and George, taking his role as chief firelighter and mood maker, to heart, has found some Christmas Carols which he is playing almost non-stop on the old record player.

It appears that the lady who owns this cottage, also loves Christmas because the book shelves host a multitude of Christmas tales and Christmas related books. I guess that they have been put here just for us. I look forward to reading them. She seems to have gone to town with the decorations too, even if some are a bit dated.

I glance at the doorway. Becky waves at me as she pins a wayward paper chain back onto the ceiling.

"I love these old fashioned Christmas decorations," she beams, "Mum, didn't we used to have fun making these when I was a child?"

Gran laughs and nods, her smile wistful. I wonder if she is thinking of Granddad Rob. The two of them move away, reminiscing about Christmases past.

I change my mind about the Dickens novel and put it back on the shelf and am about to choose another when something flashes in the corner of my eye and I hear the sound of laughter. I turn my head. No one is there. I glance at the door but Becky and Gran have moved into the kitchen. Neither seem to have heard anything. The sound whispers in the walls and fades until all I can hear is the crackle of the flames. It is odd that I am not afraid. I am curious but the noises don't scare me. They seem quite natural. I listen again but the laughter has gone.

Forgetting the books on the shelf, I tread across the rug to the fireplace. I pick up the card and trace the picture with my fingers. Glitter sticks to them and I brush it off, watching it fall to the floor like stardust. The picture's uncanny resemblance to this cottage makes me smile. What was that? A door opening? Is someone there? I pause, listening but hearing nothing. I stand the card on the mantelpiece. I close my eyes only to snap them open a moment later, hoping to surprise whoever it is who seems to be hiding from me. My heart is beginning to beat fast or is it the clock I can hear, ticking in time with the thudding in my chest?

Looking back towards the sofa I am stilled. The girl is there, blinking up at me as though I have surprised her, not the other way round. She is younger than me I now guess, ten maybe? Or perhaps she is just small for her age. She is wearing a kilt and the kilt pin gleams in the firelight. The red knitted jumper is straight from the front of one of Gran's old knitting patterns I would bet, if not older. I have seen photographs of Gran in similar outfits.

Seconds pass. I dare not breathe lest this apparition disappears. The girl does not look like a ghost. I would think her a visitor if she had not sprung from nowhere. Her feet are tucked up beneath her, just like mine were a minute ago and she looks as though she has just woken from sleep.

I am about to speak but the arrival of Buster stops me. Buster leaps onto the sofa with the girl and begins to growl at me. This is odd. What is he doing in the house? Has nobody else seen him run through? I make soothing noises and the little dog is quiet. He seems to remember me. Does he see the girl too? No sooner have I had the thought than the girl reaches out and grabs his collar.

"Shush Buster…" she says.

Her voice shocks me. It is familiar yet not familiar. What is it about her that makes me feel I know her? I am confused. The dog sits down on command and licks the girl's hand. I am staring but I can't help myself. Am I dreaming? The possibility suggests itself to me but is dismissed immediately.

I consider the facts. Buster appears to be with the ghost girl, yet yesterday, I was petting him and feeling his hot breath on my face. He was as real as I am. I am trying to work this conundrum out in my head, when Gran calls from the kitchen. Tea is ready. I don't want to leave but as I watch, the girl and the dog fade into the background and the sofa is empty once more.

"Are you all right Hannah? You look a little pale,"

"Seen a ghost then, Twig?" Joe is grinning at me. I decide not to reply.

"Ghosts?" Gran's sharp tone surprises me. I have not mentioned the girl to Gran but they all know about the dog. Becky is dishing up cottage pie and George is stretching his arms and legs in readiness. I take my place and say nothing. I think I can see Buster though, lying by the back door. He comes in and out of focus. I don't feel afraid. I am calm now and content to wait to see what will happen next.

Receiving the diary is the next strange event to occur. It is Christmas Eve morning and I am sitting on the floor of the barn, tracing patterns in the sawdust, trying to decide who I should tell about the girl and the dog or whether I should tell anyone at all. I don't know quite why I am sitting here, in the freezing cold, thinking about such things but I just feel I should be here. The feeling is so strong that I am almost scaring myself. I give myself a shake and stand up, brushing the dust from my coat.

The air has grown even colder. A shiver crawls down my spine. I can hear voices. Gran and Joe are outside, calling me. How long have I been here? I look at my watch. To my amazement an hour has gone by. I reach the door just as they are about to open it.

"Oh, there you are, we have been looking for you – come inside, there's someone here who wants to meet you,"

Gran is smiling and ushers me out of the barn and back towards the cottage. Joe is kicking at the snow and seeing him, I feel a hand of caution on my shoulder. It is my imagination, it must be. I am reading more into all this than I should but the image of the girl and the dog cannot be ignored.

The kitchen is warm and welcoming. The cherubs smile down at us. Becky is there, George is poking at the burner and feeding in yet another piece of wood.
Becky raises an eyebrow and almost drags me into the centre of the room.

"This is Hannah," she announces.

I twist out of her grip and look at the person she has addressed this amazing piece of information to. At first, her face being in shadow, it is hard to see what the woman looks like but as she leans forward to shake my hand, I give an involuntary jump. It is the same woman, the woman from the Christmas Tree yard. I check myself. No, of course, it can't be. She smiles at me. Her smile neither manic nor dazzling now, just warm and kind.

I stretch out my hand and let her shake it, for a second, before drawing back and fidgeting in discomfort. She does look like the woman in the dream but it all happened so long ago now, I could be mistaken. How many times have I thought I have seen that woman since? I chide myself for being so ridiculous.

"Hello Hannah, I wanted to meet you because your mother was saying you have been exploring the barn. I wanted to give you this," so saying, she proffers a book which I take, still puzzled as to why. Not wishing to sound rude, I thank her.

I gaze at the book and run my fingers over its leathery cover. It is small, it fits into the palm of my hand. I turn it over. The cover carries a scrawled title,

"Beatrice's Diary,"

"What is it?" I ask, curious now that I have hold of the book.

"It is a diary written by the little girl who lived here back in 1963. I thought you might like to read it, she loved playing in the barn too."

"Won't she mind?"

"Oh no, she would love you to read it. I think you will find it very interesting."

"This is Mrs Carmichael, the lady who owns Angel Cottage," Becky tells me as an afterthought. Your Gran and she are cousins. Oh, that would make you a third cousin wouldn't it?" she laughs, "She came to see you when you were born, not that you would remember of course,"

I stare at the woman who is watching me, waiting for a reaction. Am I supposed to say I do remember her? I smile, "It's good to meet you again," I say which makes them laugh. Her laugh is very like Gran's.

Ah, that must be it, Mrs Carmichael reminds me of Gran, that explains how familiar she seems. Of course, she cannot be that woman from my dreams, the woman who watched us in the car park when we picked up a Christmas tree. I feel the most ridiculous sense of relief at this realisation.

I nod to her and thank her. I am not sure what to make of the diary of a girl I never knew but she is right, I shall like to read it, even if it does feel a bit like snooping.

She reads my mind,

"It isn't like snooping at all," she tells me, "the girl who wrote it wants her diary to be read,"

"Like Anne Frank?" I ask, feeling stupid as I say it because we have just been reading Anne Frank's diary at school and I am pretty sure the diary of a girl from 1963 who played in a barn, bears no resemblance to that of a young Jewish girl in hiding from the Nazis. I stare at the missive in my hands.

She doesn't laugh at me though. Mrs Carmichael just smiles and nods.

"All girls like to write a diary but some are more telling and interesting than others," she says.

"Have you read it?"

"Yes, I have…"

I nod. Will Beatrice's diary be as interesting then? I will just have to wait and see. It would be rude to begin reading it now, though I am tempted. I wait.

Mrs Carmichael is standing up and preparing to go.

"Well, I must be off. Maybe we can all meet up before you go back home. Ray would love to say hello."

I don't know who Ray is, her husband? Gran smiles and gives her cousin a hug. They speak quietly by the door for a few minutes and then she goes but not before she has called over her shoulder to me,

"Be sure you read the diary,"

Do I detect a touch of desperation in her tone? What can be so important about an old diary?

"She hasn't changed much, since I last saw her," Becky observes as she closes the door behind our visitor, "I don't think you have seen her since before your accident George, have you?"

George looks up and shrugs. We don't often refer to George's accident, not by name. It can upset him, the mere mention bringing back terrible memories. I wonder if he will react. He doesn't. He smiles and continues to watch the flames licking at the wood behind the glass,

"She seems nice," he comments.

Becky looks at the clock.

"Lunch?" she suggests. I would rather disappear with the book but my stomach is growling. Lunch seems to be the best plan.

As soon as I can, I make my excuses and escape to the snug where I curl up on the sofa, just as the ghost girl did yesterday evening. I open the diary.

I kept a diary for a while. It was a Christmas gift from Becky and George when I was ten. I filled it in with religious fervour for the first three months. I think they thought it might help me to verbalise some of the things that made me so anxious. By the time April came, my entries were growing more sporadic and by June, I did not write in it at all.

It is evident that Beatrice was possessed of sterner stuff because as I flick through, the diary appears to have entries on almost all the pages. One thing is clear, its author loved to write. I settle back and open it at January the first.

My attention is caught by the note added at the top of the page, written in a different ink as though it was an afterthought and may have been added later. The words intrigue me. This girl, whoever she was, must have possessed a vivid imagination by the looks of things. In fact, I am wondering whether this is just a diary or if I am about to read a story. My curiosity is piqued. I read the words penned in a neat hand at the top of the page,

"They think I am mad. They think I believe in ghosts".

Chapter two

Beatrice

December 1951

I come into the world, screaming and protesting against the cold December light. It is 1951. Rationing is still in force but my mother has been eating better these past nine months than she has done throughout all the years of the war. Her family's small holding provides plentiful fruit and vegetables for us all. The posters entreating us to "Dig for victory," did not go unheard in East Devon. Hence, we are in the rudest of health given the poverty that has fallen upon so many. None of this concerns me as I glide into the world like a slippery fish.

I don't know it but I will be the middle child of three. I already have a sister, Mary, who is carried in by my father, wearing a pink knitted pram suit and carrying a blue teddy bear. She squeals when she sees me, lying in the crib by my mother's side. The midwife tut tuts and shoves my father aside, her capable hands, expertly massaging my mother's abdomen to hasten the after birth. My father thinks better of it and leaves the room for a moment.

The house is alive with the sound of activity. Downstairs, Christmas garlands are going up and the tree is being dressed. I have come into the world in a time of peace and celebration. King George V1 is on the throne, Winston Churchill has just returned to Power and the country is still preening in the wake of the Great Exhibition.

My mother is soft and warm and I lie in her embrace, cocooned in the swathe of a whiter than white shawl, knitted by Grandma Lu. Mary sits at our side and peers into my face, her wide blue eyes locking onto mine. She entwines her short fat fingers with my string like hands and the adults coo and ah, and someone fetches a Box Brownie to make the moment into history.

They don't know that the photo might never make it to delivery. The Box Brownie won't be brought back out until the summer when we go to Southend On Sea for the day and by then, the film might well have become over exposed.

Christmas comes and goes without me knowing and I live only for the softness of mother and the warm milk that flows through me from the bottle she holds to my lips. All my natural yearnings for the breast will be dismissed as my mother falls slave to current trends.

"She is the image of you, Marjorie!" declares an aunt and Marjorie preens and tucks the shawl around me so I am swaddled against her bosom.

"I can see Charles in her," she says, to make my father feel better, because I bear no resemblance in my new born state to my handsome, red haired father. Mary, on the other hand, with her titian locks and bright blue eyes that pierce right through you, is his twin.

We leave the Devon house, where Grandma Lu, growing more old and frail by the minute, waves at us forlorn, from the front gate. The front gate is adorned with angels. I will know one day that this place is Angel Cottage.

I had assumed Angel Cottage to be my home but it is not. I am taken to a big, brick built building on an estate, many miles away. My parents have made this unimposing box into a home and it boasts a twin tub washing machine and a bathroom upstairs. The cottage where I was born had no such luxury. Grandma Lu did not see the need. I will soon learn that the cottage is a place for holidays, long weekends and special occasions which we spend with Grandma Lu.

Nicholas arrives when I am a month past my second birthday. It is January at Angel Cottage. He is loud and demanding. I am relegated to no-man's land for a while as the adults coo and cluck over the scrawny, wriggling blob that is my brother. Mary and I form an alliance in those few hours, which we know will never be broken.

I love Angel Cottage. Maybe it is because I was born there, or maybe it is because I love the angels that peek out at me wherever I sit in the large, old fashioned kitchen. Grandma has no washing machine, no twin tub. She relies on the mangle and washboard she has used all her life. Her sheets billow on the line, the moisture squeezed out of them by the giant rollers.

I sit on Grandma's lap and she reads to me and I begin to pick up the words so that I am reading by myself way before I go to school. Grandma Lu says I will be a clever girl. I preen under this judgement for a while until it becomes very clear that Mary is the one with the real brains.

Mary is picked to skip a whole year aged 7. She wins a prize for science in her new form. We are proud of Mary and if I am a little jealous, I try not to show it. I read every book in the school library and am allowed to take in my own books when they run out. Even so, my light shines dim besides Mary's.

Mary wants to become a Doctor, or a scientist. She tells me this at regular intervals. I am in awe of her. She is my confidante and my partner in crime. Nicholas, younger and annoying, trails after us, miserable at times.

"Wait for me!" he calls as we race to the top of the hill opposite the lane or run down to the post box. We are not without heart and we stop and let him catch us up but he is a boy and does not share our love of secrets and gossip.

There is a barn at Angel Cottage. It used to be a working barn but it is now used for storing all manner of strange implements, some with lethal blades attached. For this reason, we are barred from entering it. It is natural, because we are barred, the place takes on a mystical air and we are not above peering through the cracks in the door now and then.

Buster joins us when I am six years old.He is a creature of "indeterminate parentage". At least, that's how Grandma Lu describes him when she meets him. I like the phrase and tuck it away for future use. I collect interesting phrases. Buster is a bundle of black and white hair with beady black eyes and a shiny nose. He must have Jack Terrier in him but he is larger than average. Mum says he has Spaniel in him too. He gets called Buster, because that's the name of the dog Mum had when she was a little girl. We are influenced by our parents in most things.

It is December 1963. We have lived here for almost six months now. That means it is more than a year since Grandma Lu died. Grandma Lu would like what we are doing to the place I think. She always complained that the cottage was cold in winter. We are putting in electric heating and an upstairs bathroom. At least, we will put them in as soon as Dad has got the money from the sale of our house in Southampton. Meanwhile, it is still the outside loo and a tin bath by the fire for us.

Mum says the cottage is in a state of flux. (I like that phrase and I intend to use it when I write my first novel). Grandma has gone, yet plenty of her remains here – the angels of course, the curtains and the rugs but there are other things you come across only as you turn out a cupboard or peer into a box. The packets of Lifebuoy soap under the sink, the sewing kit in the bureau and of course, the box of Christmas decorations that Mum says she had when she was young. Dad dragged it down from the attic this morning and Nicholas and I have been sorting through it.

It is beginning to snow which means we have to go and get the tree before the snow gets too deep. Mum has asked Nicholas to go dig one up right by the fence. Nicholas didn't moan because it is exciting digging up trees even if they are the smallest, growing just on our perimeter. It's tradition. The people who own the field behind the cottage, let Grandma choose a tree every year. We children have always helped her dig it up. My eldest sister, Mary, should come with us today but she is at a party. I should explain about Mary.

Mary is pretty with her titian hair and of course still the brightest at school and almost fourteen years old. We still do things together but she is more interested in boys and music these days. She spends hours practising her dancing in our bedroom. Sometimes I am allowed to watch and sometimes I am even allowed to join in. I like those times best of all. Mary has a record player that used to be Grandma Lu's. She drops an LP on the turntable and the Beatles blare out. If she is in the right mood, she sometimes puts the record on a different speed, so they sound like Pinky and Perky. We giggle and fall about just like we used to before she turned into a teenager and became boring.

So, it is left to Nicholas and I to fetch the tree this year. Buster, now six years old, the same age I was when we got him, gets in the way as usual. Nicholas and I are dragging the tree into the house. Buster sniffs and yelps at it as it passes. The tree looks good in its pot and even better when we have decorated it. I think we have done very well without Mary for once.

Mary comes home, flushed and excited. Mum thinks it is down to Christmas excitement. I think it is down to Gilbert Woodley. He is the reason Mary went to the party. Gilbert is one of the clever boys in the year above her. Unlike Mary, he didn't jump a year but he is a good match for her. A lot of boys find her too clever and think she is stuck up. Sometimes, I think Mary finds it all a bit much, everyone expecting so much from her all the time. I think she sometimes likes to rebel a little, which is just what she is doing today. I am just the quiet mouse who sits in her shadow. I don't mind, as a rule. Better to fly under the radar sometimes.

"The tree looks good, where's the angel?" she comments, giving it a quick once over. I am a bit miffed. Nick and I have been working hard this afternoon. We thought the star we found at the bottom of the box would do but I have to admit, I would like to see the angel on the tree too. Where can it have gone? Mum says it must have been been packed away and it will turn up. I search the box one last time, just in case we have missed it. I beg to go into the attic to see if it has fallen out but of course, I am not allowed up there on my own and everyone is far too busy to come with me. I fall into a sulk and stare out of the window at the falling snow.

It is Christmas Eve tomorrow. I hope the snow stays until then. Mum says they often used to have snow here at Christmas when she was a little girl. I imagine this place would look like a Christmas card in the snow, covered in white. Maybe like the one standing on the mantelpiece. I gaze at it, glittering beneath the soft glow from the tree lights.

Curiosity overtakes me and I stand up to take a closer look, reaching out to pick up the card and turn it over in my hand.

The words inside are scrawled in gold ink,

"Merry Christmas, with love from Hannah,"
I frown and stare at it for a moment. Why have we got a card from someone called Hannah on our mantelpiece? Who is Hannah? I am still puzzling over the identity of the sender when I hear my name being called. Replacing the card, I head for the door, the question about the card, on my lips. I don't get to ask it. Buster has managed to topple the tree and Nicholas and Mary are trying to rescue it from disaster.

It is not until the tree is restored to its former glory, or near enough, I remember the card.

"Card? Which card?" Mum asks.

"I'll get it," I tell her.

But when I go back to the mantelpiece, I cannot see it. I move the other cards aside, causing them to tumble to the floor but it appears it has vanished.

"Is this what you are looking for?"

Mary is holding out another glittery card she found on the floor beside the fireplace but it is not the one I am looking for. There is no sign of it on the floor, beneath the chairs or the sofa or indeed, in the embers of the fire that still burns in the grate. I am bemused. I am sure I saw it. I held it…I know I stood it back on the mantelpiece but perhaps it was not secure, perhaps it was blown away by a draft and maybe Buster took it off somewhere.
It seems an improbable explanation.

I am still puzzling over the strangeness of the card and of its disappearance, when we sit down to dinner but such is the way with family meals, I soon forget all about it. I don't Bring it to mind again until much, much later.

It is just before we are getting ready for bed that I see the girl. I am curled up on the sofa in the snug with a book.

"You saw a girl?" Mary is laughing at me, her voice teasing.

"Yes, she was right by the fireplace."

"Well she isn't there now, is she?"

"No, but I saw her, I did, she was standing there,"

"A ghost?" Mary's eyes are twinkling.

"Maybe, I don't know, but I saw her," it is all I can say. I did see the girl. She was standing by the fire and the next minute she had vanished. She didn't look like a ghost. At first, when I looked up from my book, I thought she was Mary. Her hair was long and looked red in the firelight. By the time I realised she wasn't Mary, she had vanished. Buster saw her too though. He was growling and I had to call him back and hold onto his collar. It all happened so fast, I can't be sure of anything except that she was there. I can tell my story doesn't sound plausible by the wry look Mary throws me,

"You must be seeing things, maybe you have a temperature?" Trust her to try and find a logical explanation. I don't feel hot. In fact, I feel quite well. Further discussion is thwarted by the arrival of Nicholas with our hot water bottles which he was asked to take to be filled.

Tucked up in bed, my feet toasting on the bottle beneath its towelling wrap, I think about the card and the mysterious girl. Are they connected? It seems possible. Have I imagined both? I am sure not. I mull over the events in my mind until I fall into a dreamless sleep.

"Bea, wake up! Wake up!" I am being shaken awake by a very excited eight-year-old. Nicholas has already pulled on his wellington boots over his pyjamas and there is a puddle of water on the carpet – melted snow.

"Have you been outside?" I am incredulous, it must be very early.

"Only by the porch – it's deep Bea, extra deep!" he is breathless with excitement.

"Ok, shush, you'll wake everyone! Give me a minute and I'll come see," I slip my feet into my slippers and grab my dressing gown to ward off the icy air that hits me as I leave the warmth of the eiderdown. Mary continues to emit gentle snores from beneath her own eiderdown.

Together, we tip toe down the stairs and lift the latch on the back door. I pull on my wellingtons and step gingerly into the deepening snow. I sink pretty much to my knees straight away and pull back with a short exclamation.

"Someone was here earlier," Nicholas tells me.

"Oh, who?"

"Dunno," he shrugs and points to the gate. It does look as though someone has left footprints on the path though they are fast being covered up by new snow.

"I expect it was the paper boy or the postman," I suggest.

"Well, he didn't get as far as the door,"

I look again. Sure enough, there are no footprints this close to the house. Perhaps he saw how deep the snow was and turned back.

"Might have just been someone out for a walk with their dog, came in to see if he was here," I say after a bit. There is no mystery here, I tell myself. In the cold light of a new day, I can convince myself that I have imagined the girl by the fireplace and I dare say I misread the name on the card too. Hannah, could have been, Anna or Harry even. Didn't Grandma have a neighbour called Harry? Anna is a friend of Mum's back at the old house.

"Hey, you two early birds, you could at least get dressed before going out. Come inside and have some breakfast!" Dad is laughing at us and holding the door open.

The day passes in comparative peace. There are no more apparitions or strange cards to be seen or found. We are hanging chocolates on the tree. It is late afternoon.

"Shall we go and look for the angel?" Mary interrupts my train of thought and I stare at her, my expression blank for a moment, "for the tree!" she elaborates.

I nod. Why not?

A trip to the attic, under Dad's supervision, proves fruitless but Mum suggests it could be in the barn. Grandma stored a lot of things in the barn and the angel might be there.

We are only too pleased to go look. The barn has always been out of bounds during Grandma's lifetime.

"Too many sharp objects in there," she used to say. It seems we are now old enough to be trusted not to decapitate ourselves with the scythe. Nicholas is allowed to come as long he doesn't touch anything and we older ones keep an eye on him.

The snow crunches beneath our boots as we cross the courtyard and Nicholas stops to roll a snowball or two. Buster is chasing snowballs and yapping in excitement. I see his yellow ball lying on top of the rain butt and pick it up, shaking off the snow and throwing it towards him. Buster leaps and catches the ball in one deft movement. Nicholas laughs and repeats the throw a few times.

"Best not let him into the barn..." Mary says. I don't know quite why but I suppose it makes sense. He might come to grief amongst all those sharp objects. Nicholas follows us having thrown the ball one last time.

"Stay there, good boy," he orders and Buster cocks his head to one side and drops the ball expectantly. Nicholas picks it up and puts it on the rain butt.

Mary and I carry on crunching through the snow until we reach the big old barn door which we heave open with no little effort.

It is dark and cold inside. We flick the switch and a pale light floods the floor. Our breath hovers in the air. We shiver despite our coats and pull our scarves up over our chins. Mary is first to the ladder. The splintered rungs travel all the way to the hayloft. A shiver runs down my spine as I look up.

"Be careful, Mary, hold on," I hear myself saying. She laughs,

"It's fine, look…" she is hanging onto the ladder with one hand, waving her free right hand at me. I wince. She knows I cannot bear heights.

"You coming up?"

I force myself to look up. She is standing at the edge of the loft now, her feet planted firm on the creaking boards. "You going up or what?" that's Nicholas. He has opened the barn door again so that cold air sweeps in. I pull my mittens further up my wrists and dig my fingers deep in the wool. He pulls the door closed, thus blocking Buster's route in.

Without a word, I make my way to the ladder and begin climbing. If I don't look down, I will be fine. This is just like going up a flight of stairs…

"Hurry up!" Mary's impatience is beginning to show. I don't think I am particularly slow but I increase my pace a little anyway. Behind me, I can hear Nicholas pawing at the ground with his boot, anxious to join us.

"Better stay there, Nick," Mary tells him. I know he will be disappointed. I can feel his disappointment boring into my back. I also know he will not stay there just because Mary says to.

With a gasp of relief, I am at the top.

"Well, what kept you?" but Mary doesn't wait for an answer, she is already lifting the lid on the trunk in the corner. I join her, kneeling on the dusty boards, pulling out the layers of tissue and exclaiming at the clothes within.

"It's a dressing up box!"

"Bea, I think it's just a box of old clothes but we could I suppose…" Mary pulls out a crocheted beret and parades around the hayloft for a moment. I laugh at her. Her red hair flies out at angles and her eyes dazzle in the dim light. My sister is beautiful, I think as I watch her.

"Ooh, look, a Box Brownie!" she is pulling out a reddish brown square object from the trunk and puts the strap around her neck, "Say cheese!" she grins,

"It's empty silly," I say but she laughs and clicks the shutter anyway. We spend five minutes adopting different poses and clicking away as though we are going to be on the cover of Vogue. I love it when Mary leaves behind all her airs and teenage moods and reverts back to the Mary I love.

"Here, catch!" she tosses something heavy and woollen towards me. I pick the garment up and give it a shake.

"It's a poncho," I grin and pull it on over my coat.

"Take your coat off first, idiot," Mary suggests, she is still clicking away as though her life depends on it.

The barn door opens and I turn to look, expecting to see Mum or Dad but instead, in walks the girl, the girl I saw by the fireplace. I stare at her but she has moved into the shadows and I can no longer tell if I have imagined her again.

I am dumbstruck as I stare at the spot she occupied a moment before, the poncho still half on and half off my head. I throw it to the floor and am about to tell Mary that the girl is back, she is here, when I see Buster clambering up the ladder, the yellow ball in his mouth. He is looking for Nicholas.

I have to step backwards to avoid Buster tripping me up.

"You let that dog in!" accuses Mary as he jumps around in excitement.

"No I didn't," objects Nick, "He's ok, look – he's just sniffing around," Nicholas has joined us in the loft despite warnings to stay put. Mary appears not to notice this disobedience. She has put the camera on the floor and is pulling out silk and satin, letting it cascade to the ground in a riot of colour. Nicholas pouts,

"What can I wear?"

"Oh, you can have this," she tosses him a battered bowler hat which he pulls on strutting around the floor, giggling to himself.

"Go away Buster, we don't want to play now," Mary admonishes and the dog trots across the barn to where Nicholas is now crouched on the floor, he seems to be inspecting the floorboards. Buster drops the ball at Nicholas's feet but Nicholas pays it little attention, kicking the ball away without looking.

"There's a loose board over here!" he is saying, as we delve deeper into the box of clothes, "This floorboard is squeaky," we take no notice.
What happens next is a blur.

Nicholas is shouting at us to look at what he has found, I just have time to notice a raised floorboard, and to see that he has picked up something that I presume has lain beneath it until now.

"Look!" he is calling, holding the something up so that we can see it. We look. Our eyes widening as we realise what it is.

"Put it down!" I think we shout this at the same time, Mary and I. Maybe we say it twice.

Nicholas doesn't have time to do anything before Buster launches his body at his master, eager to play with whatever it is that the boy is holding aloft,

"No, Buster!" I hear Nicholas caution.
There is a crash. At least I think it is a crash. I will later realise that the crash I hear is in fact the gun firing its fatal bullet. I think at first he has just dropped the thing. Then, there is a dull thud and in slow motion, I turn my head to look at my sister. Mary has dropped to the floor, a dark red patch of liquid spreading beneath her.

Nicholas has dropped the gun and is trembling. I can only sit and stare for what seems an eternity, before I realise I am screaming.

What happens next will stay with me forever, however long that may be. Our parents rush in, my mother cradling Mary's head while my father checks that Nicholas and I are all right. His eyes alight on the gun and he sees Nicholas's frightened stare but there is no time for anyone to think. The ambulance must be called and Mary is rushed to the nearest hospital. We know though, we can see, that she has gone. The bullet that fired from the barrel of the gun, shot straight through her heart. She didn't even have time to exclaim.

The Doctor is sorry, they did all they could. Auntie Jean arrives to take us children home, or rather to her home which is a good twenty miles from Angel Cottage. We go, mute with shock. Nicholas and I cling to one another in the back seat of the Morris Minor. Auntie Jean is trying to make bright conversation but her voice shakes and we know she is trying not to cry.

I want to stay at the hospital, with Mary. Even though they have explained that Mary is gone. I just cannot believe it. A policewoman has already spoken to Nicholas and me. We sat on the hard hospital chairs with our parents who could barely whisper their answers. No, they hadn't seen what happened. No, they hadn't known anything about a gun being in the barn, yes in all probability left there after the war. Yes, Mum did remember something about a German airman...Oh God, was it his gun? If it was his gun, then that means she must be to blame. I didn't understand and I still don't. What German airman and why would Mum think it her fault? I hold Nicholas's little hand, squeezing it tight in mine.

"It was my fault," he hiccups in a low, tearful voice.

The policewoman smiles at him and ruffles his hair.

"Just tell us what happened eh?" she encourages.

We tell her, both of us and she makes notes in a black notebook and says, "Uhuh," and "I see," every now and then.

"And you were the only ones in the barn at the time? You and your sister, Mary?"

We nod. Oh, and Buster of course. We tell her about Buster. We explain how Buster burst into the barn and leapt up the ladder and then launched himself at Nicholas. Nicholas couldn't help it, he was knocked off balance.

"I see, so Buster jumped up and the gun fired?"

"I think so," I shivered.

"And no one else was there?"

"No, just us."

It is only now that we are sitting in the back seat of Auntie Jean's car, that I realise that that is not quite true. There was someone else there wasn't there? Apart from Nicholas, Mary and I, there was someone else.

"The girl!" I blurt out as the car swings round a roundabout.

"What girl dear?" sniffs Auntie Jean, dabbing at her eyes with a tissue. I can see she has been crying, the way her mascara is running in lines down her face. I can see her face in the driver's mirror. Her voice is over bright. I don't think she will believe me. I glance at Nicholas. He is sobbing into his teddy bear which he clutches as though his life depends on it. Did Nicholas see the girl? I am uncertain now. Should I tell them about the girl or will they think I have imagined her? Did I imagine her? I bite my lip and stay silent.

Auntie Jean stops at Angel cottage and tells us to stay in the car while she collects some things for us, including Buster who has been locked in the house for hours. She parks the car at the foot of the drive, as far from the barn as possible. Nicholas squeezes his eyes shut as though not seeing will make it all go away. I make myself look at it. I see the barn door, now shut, as though it too has closed its eyes. It all looks so normal. I am filled with a ridiculous hope that what happened in that place, didn't happen at all. The snow has covered up all trace of our footsteps. It has covered the footprints of us children, Nicholas's, mine and Mary's – gone. So too has it covered all trace of our parents' mad dash to answer my screams and the heavy boots of the policeman who answered the 999 call. The furrows created by the ambulance are also buried beneath the new fallen mound of snow. The whole place looks pristine. I remember someone once saying how holy the landscape looks once the snow has covered all trace of existence. This is an unholy sight then. I turn away. Tears sting my eyes.

"It'll be all right," I tell Nicholas, putting an arm around my little brother and that's how Auntie Jean finds us, huddled together, sobbing without sound in the back of the car, our eyes closed against the awful spectre of that sightless barn.

Christmas Day dawns but there are no sounds of the turkey sizzling or mince pies steaming. Auntie Jean has laid the table for breakfast. Uncle Mike and our cousins, Rachel and Johnny, are already seated. Rachel is my age. She throws me a wary smile. What do you say to someone whose sister has just been shot? I smile back but there is no feeling in my bones. My smile is empty.

Uncle Mike pats our heads and winks at us. He smiles but his smile is strained and I can tell he doesn't know what to say to us. He bends down and pets Buster instead. Nicholas slinks into his chair and plays with his food. Neither of us are hungry. Auntie Jean insists we try and eat.

"Where're Mum and Dad?" I ask. It seems to me that they should be here. They can't still be at the hospital can they?

"Mum and Dad will be here later. There are things…things they have to do," Auntie Jean tells us, biting her lip.

We nod. I can't begin to imagine what needs to be done. Mary is dead — what can be done?

Johnny asks what happened.

"Johnny!" Auntie Jean admonishes.

I know she has told them not to bother us with questions but I want to talk about it. I would like to shout it out to the world except that the words fail me. I don't know how. Instead, I decide to tell them about the ghost girl.

I can tell they think I am making it up. I bet they think I have invented her just to take Mary's place. It has been less than twenty four hours since our sister died and they think I would seek to replace her with an imaginary girl? Still, I don't want them to think I am going mad so I back track and tell them I had only meant it looked like a girl. I had just imagined it. I can sense the relief in Auntie Jean's eyes. Looking after her brother's bereaved children is one thing but looking to their mental state is another.

It is only after breakfast, when we children are all sitting in the living room, staring at the unopened presents, that Rachel says anything about it.

"P'raps she was warning you, your ghost girl," she suggests.

I stare at her. She sounds as though she might even believe me. Wary, in case I am being teased, I nod and wait for more.

"It's just, I read something once, about a ghost lady who only appeared when disaster was imminent. She saved lots of people. I don't remember the details but maybe your ghost girl was like that?"

I think about it. If the girl meant to warn us she's done a pretty poor job and there was something odd about her. She didn't look very ghost like for a start. In fact, she looked quite solid and real.

Rachel and I discuss the ghost girl while the boys build a den behind the sofa. Rachel thinks the girl must have let Buster in and so she was responsible for the gun going off, not Nicholas at all. I remember the barn door opening, seeing the girl disappear into the shadows. She asks me if I have seen the girl before. I tell her about the sighting by the fireplace and the garden.

"You should find out who she is, or was," Rachel tells me.

I think about the card. Did that have something to do with the girl? It too seems to have vanished. Rachel thinks it does.

"I bet you'll find out that the girl's name was Hannah," she grins, "How exciting would that be?"

Our parents don't come back until we are all tucked up in bed. The presents under the tree remain unopened. It didn't seem right somehow, to have Christmas day today.

"We'll open them tomorrow," Auntie Jean promises. Rachel and Johnny dare not complain although I am sure they can't wait. Mary isn't their sister.

Our parents have brought back the presents that were sitting beneath the tree at home. I don't like to think how awful it was for them to leave Mary's behind. I don't ask. Nicholas is asleep before any of us.

"Exhausted," Auntie Jean says as she tucks him in like a baby. He and Johnny are sleeping head to toe in Johnny's bed. I remember sleeping like that with Mary when we used to stay with Grandma…the unasked for memory burns my eyes.

Boxing Day dawns and for a wonderful moment, I believe I am back in my own bed at home and Mary is sleeping in the bed beside me. I squeeze my eyes closed and I can hear her gentle breathing, I think I can smell her hair, spread out on the pillow like gold dust.

I turn my head but it is Rachel's gentle snoring that greets me. Her hair is the same colour as mine, a sort of dull brown that looks red in certain lights. I am on a put-you-up bed in her room.

My eyes are dry. I have cried all the tears I can for the moment. But I have woken with a feeling akin to hope. I can't explain it but it is almost as though I have a new purpose, though what that purpose is, I have yet to discover. There is a new resolve in my step as I go down the stairs. Perhaps it is just the shock setting in.

Mum and Dad hug us as though they will never let us go. They are pale and drawn. Mum looks older and dark shadows lurk beneath her eyes. Dad is red eyed and grey. I want to tell them about the girl. I want to tell them…but I don't because my resolve falters in the face of their bottomless grief. This is real. What can I offer but the imaginings of a childish mind? What difference could it make?

We try to achieve an element of normality as we open our presents. I am doing fine until I find the one that Mary wrapped for me. A small box wrapped in paper bedecked with holly. Everyone stops and stares at me as I gulp back the cry that rises up from my stomach.

I place the parcel beside me.

"You don't have to open it," whispers Mum.

I am grateful. I can't bear to read the label that Mary attached to the little box, let alone tear off the paper. I open a Judy Annual. I turn the pages. It is no good. Mary and I always read our annuals together. Where is hers? The bile in my throat threatens to spill. I excuse myself and throw up my breakfast in the bathroom.

When I emerge, Dad is there. He picks me up and cuddles me like he used to when I was much smaller and I sob into his jumper that smells of Old Spice and wood smoke.

"Shall we go back down?" he asks at last and I see that his face is wet with tears too. He hasn't shaved so stubble grazes my skin. I think of them all sitting down there.

"Can I stay here and read for a while?" I ask.

There is a bookshelf on the landing and I think how good it would be to just lose myself for a while in a random story.

"All right, but don't stay here too long, it's warmer downstairs," he tells me. I don't know what he says to those waiting downstairs but no one comes to drag me away. I am left to browse the books on the shelves my eventual choice being pulled out at random.

Glancing at the title, it appears to be about a cat. *Schrödinger's Cat. Believing I am about to read the story of a ne'er do well feline, I settle down on the rug and rest my arm on a cushion.

Quantum theory is not something I am familiar with but by the time I am finished reading, something has changed, something within me has come alive.

I put the book down and stare at it for a while. I have re-read part of it several times. It all sounds so feasible to me. I sit here for a while, my mind trying to make sense of what I have just read. It is only when the cold creeps into my fingers that I decide to move into the bedroom which is where Rachel finds me, a couple of hours later, snuggled beneath the eiderdown on the put-you-up, the book cradled in my arms. I am staring at the door.

"What are you doing? Oh, that's one of Dad's books…is it good?" she asks, reading the title in surprise.

"It's…interesting," I tell her. I pat the bed and she sits down with me, crawling beneath the eiderdown for warmth.

It is comforting to have her there, where Mary might have been, where Mary might be still. The eiderdown wraps itself around us and keeps out the draft. We lie there for a while, enjoying the warmth. Our breath makes little clouds in the air around us. I can hear Aunt Jean rattling teacups in the kitchen and our parents trying to make bright conversation. It all seems surreal. Rachel clasps my hand and I realise tears are pouring down my face again.

"Do you really believe in ghosts?" I sniff at last, with a sudden desire to know.

Rachel frowns, it is clear she is wondering where this is leading. I imagine she thinks I am about to suggest a séance or something.

"Maybe, yes," she says, dragging the words out, "I believe you saw someone in the barn, so I suppose I must do."

I haven't explained my theory to her yet. Indeed, I haven't explained it to myself. I take a deep breath and pick up the book. It seems as good a place to start as any.

"I think the barn is like the box in Schrödinger's Cat," Rachel looks from the book to me in askance.

I nod at the page I have opened it to. I want her to see, I want her to understand, I want her to agree with me, I begin to read aloud,

"The cat is put into a box with a radioactive sample and a Geiger counter and a bottle of poison. The box is sealed. If the radioactive material decays, the poison bottle breaks and the cat dies. The theory is, until someone opens the box and checks, the cat is neither dead nor alive or is alive and dead at the same time."

I can see I have lost her. Not surprising at all. I am not getting my point across very well. I have spent hours reading this text over and over again. Is it my over active imagination that is making something out of nothing? I push the book towards her,

"Here, you read it, that bit, about the box…?"

She takes the book from me and concentrates. The furrow in her brow deepens. I wait as nervous as someone waiting for the results of a test. I watch as her eyes scan the page.

After a bit, she begins to read aloud.

> The hypothetical experiment, was devised by the physicist in 1935. In it, a cat is placed in a sealed box together with a radioactive sample, a Geiger counter and a bottle of poison.
>
> If the radioactive material decays, the Geiger counter will detect it and will trigger the smashing of the bottle of poison. The cat will be killed.
>
> The experiment was supposed to illustrate the flaws of the 'Copenhagen interpretation' of quantum mechanics, which states that a particle exists in all states at once until observed.

"So, what you are saying is…" Rachel pauses, eager not to misunderstand the thing I have taken such pains to describe., "The cat can be both alive and dead at the same time? Depending on whether something happens or not and if that something is seen to happen?"

I nod.

"But what has this got to do with your ghost girl?"

"It's a similar situation…"

"But the book says Schrodinger made that up to disprove something else didn't he?"

I nod again, biting my lip,

"Yes, but he has made me look at it all in a different way. Think of it like this Rachel, if the barn becomes that box, the gun is the poison and Mary is the cat… the Ghost Girl coming into the box is a random event which causes the gun to fire. The girl saw Mary fall, I am pretty sure of that. If she hadn't come into the barn, maybe the gun would not have fired," I pause, eager to say the next bit as calmly as possible, "So, if we could stop her going into the barn, the gun would not fire and Mary would not be shot."

At last, I stop and allow her to speak,

"But it has happened, she was there, we didn't stop her and it's in the past, I don't understand…"

That's just it Rachel. It happened in our past but is it in hers? Suppose this girl isn't a ghost from the past at all? Suppose she comes from the future?"

My words sound strange as though uttered by someone else. I wait for Rachel's response.

"Let me see it again," she says and goes back to the book.

I wait, watching the concentration on her face as she scans the pages. I see the way she curls her bottom lip behind her teeth. I judge the moment to be right to speak,

"So, if I did see this girl and we agree that I did and if she is not a ghost from the past but came from the future…then in her time, maybe she hasn't been there yet. She hasn't seen Mary fall yet and Mary only falls when the girl sees her. That means, it hasn't happened yet…it isn't history. Maybe there is still time to stop her from opening the barn door and letting Buster in. Maybe…" I pause, my voice cracking now, "…maybe Mary is still alive."

Rachel's brow furrows again and she chews this over for a moment.

As preposterous as my words may sound, I am sure now. The thing that has bothered me about the ghost girl who wasn't a ghost, is clear now, she was too alive, too present. Her clothes, her hairstyle…none of it fitted with the past, not even the recent past. I am certain.

"The girl was from the future," I repeat.

"Wow!" Rachel breathes, her frown deepening. Have I lost her again? Was she willing to believe in ghosts from the past but not from the future? I don't want to lose her. I need her to believe me. I need this to be true. I try again,

"Look, if the girl, we'll call her Hannah, because of the card, is from the future, that means she travelled back in time. It is quite possible she isn't even born yet. You said it is her fault the gun went off. Think of that Rachel. Hannah doesn't exist at the moment so how can she have been there? She still has to be born and somehow travel back in time and walk into the barn on Christmas Eve in our time by some quirk of fate. But she has to do this in her time," I pause, a triumphant gleam in my eye, "And that would mean that Mary is still alive somewhere...waiting." I watch as her eyes open wide at the thought, I push on when I see understanding begin to dawn, "When your Mum took us to fetch our stuff, I was looking at the barn. It looked, untouched, it looked, sealed."

"Like the box? Look Bea, this could be something, you know? If this ghost girl is from the future...that means, if you could find her and stop her from going into the barn, things might be different."

I nod. It's not only far-fetched, even if it is true then the chances of me finding the girl seem pretty slim, given that I have no idea where in the future she came from. I ignore this fact for the time being. I don't want to cast doubt on something that I have only just understood myself.

"Quite," I agree. I am already thinking what I would ask the girl to do if I found her. Perhaps she could remove the gun before Christmas Eve or at the very least, stop Buster from leaping at Nicolas. I pick up the copy of Schrödinger's Cat and clasp it close. It seems to hold the key to everything.

"You can keep that if you like," Rachel says, "Those books are from the second-hand bookshop, we swap them all the time. That one won't be missed. I will help you. We can find her, Bea, I am sure of it.

I clutch the book close, the back cover towards me, the words now etched on my brain.

"The scenario presents a cat that may be simultaneously both alive and dead - a state known as a **quantum superposition**, as a result of being linked to a random subatomic event that may or may not occur."

It all makes sense in some wild and outlandish way. Mary is linked at random to an event that cannot be explained by normal physics, the appearance of someone from the future. Something that it is clear is not meant to happen, has had a catastrophic effect on our present. If that random appearance can be changed because it has yet to happen, Mary may well live and our lives will go on as before. I am so sure of this by the time we have finished talking, that I am almost willing to bet my life on it, Mary's too. The bottom line is, if on one level, the random act has yet to take place then it can be changed. Rachel's expression matches my own. It is one of purpose.

As we close the bedroom door behind us, we link our little fingers,

"Soulmates," we say, sombre as we look at one another, each understanding the other without a need for further words. I know we have just agreed to a colossal task.

It is past suppertime when Rachel and I are able to talk about the ghost girl, who is not a ghost girl, again. By this time, I am feeling the first real surges of hope.

"So, have you thought any more about her, the girl you saw, about Hannah?" Rachel asks, as we squeeze into the space between her bed and the chest of drawers, where the hot water pipes run beneath the floorboards, our knees drawn up to our chests.

I like that she has named the girl. Why shouldn't that be her name? The Christmas card, the sightings, they all tie in.

"Of course, I have been trying to think about what she was wearing and what she looked like, so I don't forget. I don't tell her that I have also been trying to remember what Mary looked like when I last saw her alive. A corner of my mind seems closed to me. It is this corner I need to unlock if I am ever to have a hope of finding Hannah.

"Did you remember anything then?" Rachel prompts, eager to hear.

I nod, my expression grave, picturing the girl by the fireplace in our sitting room back at the cottage. What was she wearing? There was something distinctive I know, but what?

"I'm not sure, I need to get it straight in my mind before I tell you," I tell my cousin.

Rachel nods,

"That's all right Bea. Bea?"

"Yes?"

"It is possible isn't it? I keep thinking, we haven't just dreamt this up?"

"Well, I know I haven't dreamt it. I know I saw this girl whatever her name might turn out to be and I know, I just know Rachel, don't ask me how, but I know if we can find this girl, we can change things."

"Of course, if we change things, if we bring Mary back, then we won't ever have had this conversation will we? We might not even have been together today."

This is only the first of many 'what if' moments we will have. A shiver travels from my spine to my fingertips. The two of us lock fingers again, soulmates.

Our stay with Auntie Jean and Uncle Mike is for longer than planned. It seems Mum and Dad cannot bear the thought of going back at the cottage.

"We'll go back after the funeral," Mum says.

The funeral is held just after New Year. The snow melted on Boxing Day. Since then it has become even colder. It seems that with Mary's death, everything decent and nice has left this world. It is a bleak and unforgiving wintery day. The wind whips my hair across my face so that I can't see and stings my eyes. I am glad she is warm in that coffin. I don't want to think of what will happen to her once she is under the earth. I imagine her sleeping forever, wearing that pale blue dress that mother chose for her.

The church is packed with local well-wishers. There are red and gold Chrysanthemums on the coffin. The vicar is very kind and talks about a young life ending too soon, a tragic accident, then he mentions Nicholas and I and we feel all eyes turn upon us.

"Mary's brother and sister will miss her but they will provide welcome solace for their parents, Marjorie and Charles," and addressing us, "It is up to you two, to go out into the world and carry on. Mary would want to see you succeed.

I squirm in my seat and Nicholas is rigid with fear, the vicar continues,

"Mary was destined for great things, she was bright, intelligent and I believe she would have gone on to greater things. Her loss will be felt by us all but we know she is now in the arms of Jesus…"
I stop listening.

"It was my fault," whispers Nicholas as the curtains close around the coffin and the music plays.

"No, it wasn't!" I hiss but I know he doesn't believe me.

Everyone goes back to Aunt Jean's afterwards. She has laid on sandwiches and tea. Rachel and I sneak upstairs and sit, in our starched black skirts, on the linoleum by the heating pipes. Feeling the warmth seep into our bones. We giggle. It seems wrong to be giggling like this when everyone has been so sad but we can hear the grownups laughing as they recall something Mary did or said. It is the sort of laughter borne from grief though, the kind that bubbles up in place of tears. Rachel and I hug our knees and talk about Hannah and the possibility of changing history. With the reality of Mary's death sinking in, I am clinging with a hint of desperation to this idea. I don't know whether or not I believe it, deep down. Rachel seems to or is she just humouring me? I don't know. All I do know is, the pain is eased when I immerse myself in this fantasy.

"You have to go back some time Marjorie," Aunt Jean is cajoling as we walk into the conservatory. Mother is tapping her fingers on the arm of the chair. She looks thinner. Black does not suit her, it drains her of any colour. Behind her, my father is talking to one of the old aunts. This one is a little deaf and he has to shout to be heard.

"What's that?" she says, frowning and craning her neck upwards. My father is tall so this is not easy. He stoops a little so that she can hear him better.

"Are you cold?" he repeats,
Great Aunt Philippa, waves him away,

"Well I know it's because I am old but it is rather rude to say so," she mutters.
My father raises an eyebrow and then winks at me. Once I would have enjoyed this comic scene and would have entered into the spirit of it by winking back. Now, I feel numb, empty of mirth.

"We'll make plans tomorrow," mother says and Aunt Jean nods.

"Good, you need to get back into the swing of things. You can't mope around Marjorie, Mary wouldn't have wanted that, you have two other children to worry about."

"Yes, I know but ..." Mum spreads her hands in a hopeless gesture and my heart somersaults.

I may be convinced that finding Hannah will change things but for now, the grief is real and Mary is not with us. I have to admit that I have no idea how long this quest might take and in the meantime, we have to deal with things as they are. The numbness stays with me but the new resolve keeps me going.

Nicholas has become withdrawn. He hasn't said much since we got here.

I hear whispered conversations between my parents. For the most part, it is Dad trying to console Mum. She keeps insisting it is all her fault. I cannot see how but she is adamant. It is not until I find the diary that I begin to understand.

"Keep in touch!" begs Rachel, as I climb into the car for the drive home. Nicholas is sullen and says little all the way home. Mother tries to get him to laugh but it is useless. Things don't improve once we are home. Mum cries a lot and Dad doesn't say anything for a long time afterwards. Nicholas and I go up to our room – we share mine now that Mary has gone. It is comforting. It started with Nicholas crawling into my bed in the middle of the night at Aunt Jean's when he couldn't sleep. When we were back at Angel Cottage, it was a natural progression for him to move his things in to my room.

Now, we sit on my bed and look through the pile of Christmas cards that Mum took down when we got home. The decorations have been thrown into the box and Buster sets up a constant whine, uncertain of his place now in this dysfunctional family.

Mum seems bound to get worse before she gets any better.

"It's natural," Aunt Jean insists when she visits, "You must give her time, you all need time."

The Doctor prescribes sedatives but still Mum lies awake crying at night and Dad is so worried about her that he takes more time off work until his firm make the tactful suggestion that he take unpaid leave.

Now they are both in the house all day long. The atmosphere is thick with grief. They are talking about moving.

"We have to get on with things," Dad insists. I hear him sigh.

They try then, we can see how hard they are trying to make things normal for us but living here, where it all happened, isn't easy. No one goes into the barn. I think someone, one of the neighbours maybe, came in and cleaned it when we were away. I don't like to think about that but the blood on the floor...that couldn't just be left. I won't go back in there for a very long time. To me it is a place of horror.

For a while, I forget all about the ghost girl and the possibility of us ever being able to change things. There is only now and now is almost unbearable.

The new term begins. We go back to school and receive pitying looks from our classmates and teachers. I pretend a brightness I do not feel and they say how well I am handling it. Nicholas, on the other hand, doesn't want to go to school after the first week.

We find out he has been bullied. Some of the boys in his class are saying he killed his sister. Our parents have to go up to the school and are told things will settle down. Something else will come along to distract the bullies. But the damage has been done.

Nicholas gets into fights and stops trying in his lessons. He starts playing truant and gets into trouble. His behaviour is causing our parents concern.

I try and protect him as much as I can but we are in separate buildings at school. I see him from my classroom window sometimes, facing up to the bullies but still very much alone when they have gone. Where are his friends? I would do anything to stop him hurting. I am angry at Mary for leaving us. Not everyone dies who gets shot do they?

Uncle Alfie got shot in the war and he survived, he has a limp but he didn't die, did he? You hear of people being shot and recovering all the time don't you? Why did Mary have to be the one who died from it? I jab the potato with my fork and get rebuked for playing with my food.

Buster whines at my feet and I pet him without thinking, feeling his hot dry tongue on my hand.

"Don't pet the dog at the table please," my father says. Can I do anything right? I bet he wouldn't tell Mary off for petting the dog at the table.

"Beatrice!" that's mother. Did I say that aloud? It appears so because they are both ordering me up to my room. Well, at least they are communicating with one another, I think as I climb the stairs and slam the door behind me.

Alone in my room, I laugh at myself. My behaviour is ridiculous. I am acting like a spoilt brat. What is happening to me? This isn't how I want to be. I look over at Mary's bed in which Nicholas now sleeps. He has brought his blue eiderdown in. Her pink one is nowhere to be seen. I stand at the window and stare across to the barn.

Can it be true? I want to see the girl again. I want to know that she did exist. The garden is empty. Buster is chasing a robin. He'll never catch it. He spots his ball and picks it up, running round and round until he is exhausted and flops down, panting on the frozen ground.

I can hear voices floating up from the kitchen.

"She's hurting, just like us," that's mother.

"It's not her I am worried about, it's Nicholas. He doesn't speak! I think we need to seriously consider moving, we can't move on with our lives while we stay here." My father is right.

I want to tell them about the girl. But they will wonder why I didn't speak up before won't they? I mull it over and over in my mind. They will think I am mad. They will put it down to the imaginings of an overactive mind or wishful thinking. I shan't tell them. Rachel and I will keep this secret.

"I won't give up though," I tell the photograph of my sister that sits on my bedside table.

As I lie in my bed at night, their voices rise and fall as they discuss their options. I look across at Nicholas. He is always awake, clutching his teddy and biting his lip.

"It's my fault," he whispers, again and again. I slip out of my bed and slide in beside him. Together, we lie there and listen to our parents' muffled voices echoing up the stairway. One night we hear them say they have found somewhere, a more modern house in town.

Gilbert comes across with a card and some flowers for our mother. Red rimmed eyes peer out from behind thick spectacles and he sniffs when he hands the flowers to me. He doesn't look like the handsome young man Mary mooned over. He looks like a lost little boy. I bet his mother slicked his hair down before he left the house.

"Sorry, for what's happened," he says and I think he might start bawling there and then. Something inside me twists. I stand up tall, as tall as a twelve-year-old can.

"Thank you, they are very nice," I tell him, using my most formal voice. The words sound lame even to my ears but I can't think of any others. Mother comes to my rescue. She takes the flowers and manages to smile at Gilbert and to talk to him for several minutes. He regains his composure and comes in for a hot chocolate. That's weird, Gilbert being there. I don't think he has ever been in for a hot chocolate before. Nicholas and I sit at the table too. Mother puts three large mugs in front of us and we sip them.

"How's your mother?" she asks.

The questions are so banal, so trite. I look at her in surprise. Her eyes are hollow but she still smiles, she still attempts to be normal.

Nicholas doesn't say much at all about anything. He stirs the hot chocolate with his finger, bringing a sharp rebuke from Mother.

I see the look that Gilbert gives him. I think I can read his mind. He is thinking, is that the boy who pulled the trigger? Did he kill Mary?" I feel his pain. Then I see him with new eyes again and he is that sad little boy. Poor boy.

"What's wrong Beatrice?" Mother is asking. The question startles me. I had not realised I had said anything out loud but I must have done because they are all looking at me.

"Oh, nothing, sorry," I mumble.
I wonder what it is I said. They stare at me for a moment before mother changes the conversation.
"Where did you go for Christmas?" she asks.
Gilbert shrugs,

"We went to my Gran's. Mum thought it might be best after…everything…" he admitted. I could understand that. We had stayed at Aunt Jean's for the very same reason. At the thought of Aunt Jean, I also remembered the conversation with Rachel. That first tentative one, when we had agreed to believe in something so ridiculous that under normal circumstances, I'd have laughed it off the table.

"We might be moving." I say.

"Are you? Where to?" he is relieved I think, feeling uncharitable as I gaze back at him. He won't have to look at us every day and remember. We won't have that luxury. Every day we will see ourselves and wonder if we could have stopped it. That's the thought that dogs my sleep and keeps me awake at night. What is it that I could have done to stop this from happening? Since speaking to Rachel and reading that book, I believe there is something I can do, some day, to change things but right now, my soul is being torn apart by grief.

"Into town," I reply.

"Oh,"

"You can visit," I make the offer knowing that he won't. Why would he?

"Yeah, ok," he smiles.

"Well, you must give our best to your mother and tell her I will pop round before we leave."

Gilbert takes the hint and stands up, placing his empty cup on the draining board.

"Thank you, Mrs Dean," he says.

I walk him to the door. After all, I am the eldest now.

"She was lovely, your sister," he mumbles as we go to the door. I warm to him a little then. I touch his arm before he leaves,

"Yes," I agree.

"Well, wasn't that nice of him?" Mother is saying in a voice a little too bright. She is arranging the flowers in a vase, Chrysanthemums, seasonal favourites. We put Chrysanthemums on Mary's coffin. I push the image away and try to replace it with one more pleasing. I struggle to find one.

"Well we have found somewhere, we are moving," Mum confirms a few days later when we are gathered in the sitting room before tea.

"Moving?"

Now that it is going to happen, I can't imagine moving from here. It will be like leaving Mary all over again, the room we shared, the garden we played in, the barn where...I haven't thought about the ghost girl for a while but I do now.

"We can't move," I say, panic gripping me.

Mum smiles and gives me a squeeze, "We won't go far but a different house, somewhere with less sad memories…your Dad has got a job in Lanscott. It's only a few miles away. It'll be a new start."

"Will we go to different schools?"

"Yes, it'll be a chance for you, Nicholas to settle down,"

I can't argue with that can I? It will be good for Nicholas I am sure. What about the ghost girl though? If we don't live at the cottage, how will she find us? I think about it for a bit. If my theory is right, then she is living at the cottage at some point in the future. Perhaps we have to move so that she can come here. I mull this over for a while.

"Will we sell Angel Cottage?" I ask the question but one look at into my mother's eyes and I already know the answer, they will never sell this place. They might not be able to live here but sell it? No!

"We will keep it on but your Dad thinks we could let it out, maybe to holiday makers," she tells us. I am appalled. The thought of strangers tramping through our rooms, strangers in the barn…

"We won't give anyone access to the barn. It's too soon," Mum has read my thoughts it seems. I consider these facts for a while. It is clear that Hannah did get into the barn or I would never have seen her there. Whether I stay or go can't affect that can it?

I nod my assent though they will do what they think best regardless of what I say. Mum and Dad say, "Jolly good," and that seems to be that.

We begin packing up for the move.

We will be out by Easter. I am glad about that. I have been dreading another Christmas in this place. The thought of choosing a tree from the forest, decorating it without Mary being there… it is too horrible to even think about. Before that, I have a whole summer to get through without her of course. It will be easier to do that somewhere else where there aren't so many reminders.

The hardest part in all this, is having to pack Mary's things away. I tell myself it is only temporary. One day, we will wake up and all this will have been a bad dream. This is the way I cope. This is the way I manage to make the transition from the cottage to the small but tidy, house in town.

I have high hopes for Nicholas when we move to Lanscott. We all do. These past few months have been hard for him but now, in a new place, it must be possible for him to leave the awful memories and the guilt behind him.

Just before we move, I hear our parents talking late one night about my wayward brother.

"He blames himself but it wasn't his fault, we know it wasn't," Mum is saying.

"Of course, it wasn't his fault Margie, but neither was it yours. You have got to stop blaming yourself for something you had no way of knowing about."

"But I should have known, I should have remembered about the gun...don't you see? I am to blame..." her voice is low and tearful. Dad sounds exasperated as he tries to placate her. I wonder what on earth she is talking about.

I don't think Nicholas is to blame but did Mum know the gun was there and if so, how did it get there? I am determined to ask. Now is not the time though. Their voices rumble on for some time before I hear the sound of doors being closed and lights being switched off. I wait until the house has gone quiet before I dare close my eyes.

The diary comes into my possession when we are clearing the attic. A box of books, brought down to be sorted through, reveals several old annuals and paperbacks and what looks like a small, plain notebook. Grandma Lu was fond of writing in such notebooks. We have found them secreted in drawers and cupboards, full of shopping lists, recipes and gardening tips. At first, I assume it to be one of these. Mum says they are not worth keeping. This one is different. The initials on the cover, M.E.W Marjorie Elizabeth Wilson tell me it belongs to my mother.

A quick scan of the pages and I know it to be a diary of sorts. The pages have been ruled into sections. From what I can see, it was written in 1943. How intriguing! I read the first couple of entries. Nothing amazing here. She writes about life on the farm for this was a small farm back then.

My imagination sees her running down to the meadow to feed the pigs or swilling out the stables behind the barn. I picture her running down the lane to meet her friend Millie so that they can go to school together and I feel I can tell how she felt when her brother, Alfred, was reported missing, presumed dead. I know of course, that he was later found alive if not well, in a prisoner of war camp and now lives in Bridlington but she is so sad on those pages when they thought him lost. I feel for her.

It is a strange experience to find yourself looking at your mother as she was when she was a young girl. I have seen photographs of course. This is different. This is something she wrote when she was not much older than I am now. She was about Mary's age in fact. I do a quick mental calculation. Reading this is a bit like reading something Mary would have written, I am sure.

I don't read it all at first of course. I intend to give it to Mum and ask her about it but then, she is busy and Dad tells us to give her some peace. Curious, I retreat to the snug and curl up on the sofa with my find.

The entries dwindle towards the middle of the year, only picking up pace again as Autumn approaches. She writes of being able to see the distant dog fights,

"We can see the flashes of the gunfire in the distance and planes roar overhead en-route to Bristol."
I shiver at the thought.

"Enemy bombers have been shot down off Falmouth harbour. Everyone has been told to be on the look-out for the enemy."

It is like reading a fantastic novel but this was all too real for my mother. It is almost dark as I turn the page to read December's entries.

By the time I am finished, I understand. I understand why my mother blames herself, whether it is right or wrong and I understand why the gun was there. I feel tears building behind my eyes but they are tears of anger, anger that that young airman should think it safe to leave his gun there for Nicholas to find, loaded and ready to fire.

Blinded by my anger I jump up and run into the living room, waving the notebook in the air.

"It's Heinrich's fault! All of it, Heinrich's fault! I hate the Germans!" I scream.

My outburst shocks both my parents into the realisation that I have not only found the diary but I have read it.

"Oh, my goodness!" my mother's hand is clamped to her mouth.

"Now give me that, Beatrice, come here, it's ok, it's ok," Dad's voice, comforting as he grabs my arms and gathers me to him, a sobbing, jelly-like mess.

When my sobs subside I manage to look at her, my mother. She is now holding the diary in trembling hands.

"It wasn't your fault," I manage between hiccups. She shakes her head.

"Oh Beatrice, I should have known, I should have checked but your Grandma, she told me she had dealt with everything. I didn't know there was a gun hidden there. But I should have done. He didn't have it when they took him did he?" she appeals to my father who shrugs and blinks back his own tears.

"The sooner we leave all this behind the better," he mumbles.

Chapter three

December 1943

Marjorie

The day begins like any other December day. Mummy dishes up porridge from the big old saucepan, for the two of us, just as she does every morning. Mine is gloopy and I feel it sticking to the roof of my mouth. My face must bely my distaste.

"Be grateful, there are plenty not getting food on the table at the moment," she bites her lip, "I dread to think what poor Alfie is eating right now, if anything. Stuck over there in a French field, facing German bullets," she stops short, the thought too painful to consider."

I feel instant remorse. God knows what poor Alfie is having right now.

"Well, send him some of this porridge for ammunition, put that in a cannon and it'd soon fight off any German bullets," I say, in a weak attempt to make her smile.

She pretends to be cross but I see her mouth curl up at the corners as she sticks her spoon into the gloop,

"Maybe it is a little…stiff," she concedes after a while. We go back to our normal routine – we eat, she washes the dishes while I dry.

"It's beginning to snow again," she observes when we have put the plates away and are sitting at the table, peeling the vegetables for dinner. (she likes to get this finished in good time so she can get the other chores on the farm done). Of course, it is not a farm any more, not in the real sense. We grow a few vegetables and we keep some chickens, we used to have a couple of milk cows but we sold them to "Beastly Eastly," as I call Mr Eastly, last year.

With no men around, we decided we'd dig for Britain like Mr Churchill wants. We make enough from selling the vegetables to keep us going and we are quite self-sufficient on the whole. When Alfie was here, he snared the occasional rabbit. I can't bear to do that but we had pheasant in the autumn. We do all right.

I follow her gaze. It has been threatening to snow all morning. A smattering fell last night but disappeared when the sun rose. The sky looks heavy now. Large flakes begin to fall even as I watch. Within minutes, it is falling thick and fast. I watch as the flakes merge into one. In no time at all the grass and path are white and the dustbin is fast being buried. Within half an hour, the garden is hidden beneath its snowy blanket and there is a blizzard raging outside. I stare out of the window as I slice a large carrot into chunks.

"You'll cut your fingers off if you are not careful," she warns.

It is all so normal, as normal as life can be in these times of course. The air raids on the cities have worsened and everyone moans about the rationing. Here in the countryside, we are told to be on the look-out for Germans infiltrating our villages. Daddy and Alfie have both been gone for months and we have had no word from Alfie since September. Daddy is at the War Office in London. We don't know what he is doing apart from the fact that he can't come home very often.

I drop the carrot into the bowl and move to the sink from where I can see the field beyond. Something has caught my attention.

At first, I think it is a large white bird that I spy diving into the trees but the large white bird appears to have stopped, hanging in mid-air and I realise, with a surprised gasp, that it is not a bird at all but a parachute.

Mother has seen the spectacle at the same time as me. She is already running to the door, I think at first to lock it. If this is a German invader, shouldn't we be hiding in the cellar? Mummy has other ideas. She has already pulled on her coat and boots. Grabbing a broom (why a broom?) she rushes out of the door and tells me to stay where I am. Of course I do no such thing, I pull on my boots and grab my coat, running after her.

The chute has landed across the lane, in the clump of trees about fifty yards away. I think of all the talks we have listened to at school, what we should do if we ever find ourselves in such a situation. None of them recommend running out of the house with a broom.

"Marjorie!" Mummy hisses when she catches sight of me charging after her. I pull up short and grin. Snowflakes land on my lips and in my hair, I shake them off but they are replaced by more. It's Mummy and me against the world or against the Germans in this instance.

"I think he's stuck in the tree," she whispers. We are peering through the shrubbery and can just see someone dangling from the parachute which appears to have become entangled in the branches of the old oak tree. Alfie and I used to sit in that tree and watch the world go by so I am pretty sure we have been spotted.

"Do you think there are more of them?" I glance round, nervous of what I might see.

"Stop looking so worried. He's just a boy, no more than Alfie's age,"

I stare at the boy who hangs there, watching us with wary eyes. He is attempting to free himself from the chute and mother rushes forward calling to him to be careful. It is a perilous drop to the ground. This only serves to make him struggle more and in an instant he has divested himself of the encumbrance and plummets to the floor, wincing as he hits terra ferma.

We watch as he attempts to stand and with a cry, falls back to the ground, clutching his ankle. We begin a slow shuffle towards him, neither sure of our own safety because despite his apparent injury, he may have a gun or a grenade. On the other hand, this could all be a ploy and he is not injured at all.

We are within touching distance of him now and he is not pretending to be hurt, that much is clear. His ankle is twisted at a cruel angle and the grimace on his face is real.

Mother ignores him and goes to where the parachute blows in the wind. It would be seen from the road if anyone drives by. She uses the broom to dislodge the rope and lower the chute to the ground. It is still attached to the tree but at least it is no longer waving around for all to see, she tells me.

"Marjorie," she says, pointing to the young airman, "Help him to his feet, we must get him back to the house,"

I am open mouthed. Should we not call Sergeant Steele? This is the enemy in front of us although he looks no more than a child. In spite of these thoughts, I shuffle towards him and offer my hand. He looks up at me and I am struck by both the blueness of his eyes and the fear held within them. My heart melts.

"Come," I say and offer my hand again. At last he seems to decide that I am not going to hurt him and allows me to help him to his feet. He cannot support his weight on both so we hobble back to the house, while mother attempts to drag the parachute across the field and hide it in the ditch.

In the house, I guide the German Airman to a chair where he collapses against the cushions with a sigh.

"Heinrich," he says, tapping his chest weakly. He looks exhausted. Mother puts a bowl of soup in front of him. He guzzles it in an instant. The bread she places before him is gone in the same amount of time. When he has finished, he sits back, his eyes darting round the room, alighting on the photograph of my father and my brother, taken just before they went off to war, proud in their uniforms. I wonder what he is thinking.

Later, when we have made him comfortable I take out my diary. This is too good a story not to write down.

It is so amazing, I am not sure I know how to write it. There is a German airman in our barn. We found him hanging from a tree in the field opposite the cottage. Mummy and I saw him. He is very young, even younger than Alfie. I think that's why Mummy felt we should look after him. We hope that someone would do the same for Alfie. Poor thing was frozen through. The snow is quite heavy today. All the phone lines have been brought down.

Heinrich is very good looking for a German. Not at all like the soldiers in the newsreels, with their weird marching and those mean looking helmets. He looked very scared hanging there. We managed to cut him down but he has injured his foot and can't walk so we half carried him to the house. He wasn't very heavy. Mummy thinks he hasn't been eating much and she gave him half our beef stew. He speaks a little English. Mummy says she will phone the authorities as soon as the lines are up again. That means Sergeant Steele I expect.

I persuaded Mummy to let me take Heinrich his supper. She told me not to hang around, it's not good for me to spend too much time with him but I think she was pleased I wanted to help. She is so busy with everything on the farm now that Alfie and Daddy have gone away. We had to go back for the parachute which Mummy has put in the barn for the time being. She says she will give it to the authorities.

December 20th

Heinrich smiled at me. He has the bluest eyes and the loveliest smile – I think I might be in love. I made sure I collected his empty plate and was amazed at how much he could eat. Mummy said it looked as though he had licked the plate clean.

Mummy says Heinrich can't stay in the house. He has to go into the barn to sleep. She thinks it will be safer there for him. I think she just wants to make sure I don't spend too much time with him. I carried the lantern for him and we helped him across the yard.

There is plenty of hay in the loft - that's one thing Daddy made sure of before he left this time. I took out my spare quilt and made it snug for him. I gave him one of my books to read but I don't think he understands it. He was very grateful though. Mummy wasn't impressed, she said we shouldn't give him anything but food and medical care. I know she gave him a hot water bottle though and I saw her face when he thanked her.

December 21st

It is almost Christmas. Mummy says she has to try and contact Sergeant Steele today. It seems we could be in big trouble if we don't report Heinrich. The problem is the phone lines are still down what with all the snow. The road is impassable and Mummy won't leave me here alone with the German boy. His ankle is a bit better today and he is hobbling around using a stick he found in the barn. I found him talking to the chickens earlier.

It is eerie round here at the moment … so quiet.

December 22nd

Well, it's been a weird day. First, Heinrich helped Mummy chop some wood in the yard. Then a tractor drove up and Mummy told him to go inside. It was Mr Eastly from Brock's Farm. He had come to see if we were all right. Mummy didn't say anything about Heinrich. She says Mr Eastly is a mean sod. I don't know how that can be since he is being so nice to us but she says he is just buttering us up, hoping to get his hands on the farm, with Daddy away. I don't know about that but I do know Mummy did not tell him about Heinrich. "Wouldn't give him the satisfaction!" she muttered when I asked her.

December 23rd

It is Christmas Eve tomorrow. Heinrich drew a picture of his home and family for me. I gave him the photo of me with Alfie taken last summer. He said he couldn't take it but he looked at it and held it to his heart. Oh, I am sure I am falling in love!

December 24th – Christmas Eve

Things couldn't be worse here. The phone lines have been fixed and Mummy phoned the police station from the phone box. Sergeant Steele and PC Blake, walked all the way here from the village, in the snow, which is piled up either side of the lane in 6 foot drifts. They told us that a German plane ditched off Falmouth Harbour the other night and someone saw a parachute falling somewhere over this way. They have been searching.

I sort of hoped that Mummy was going to keep our secret but she said she couldn't keep quiet.

"It's one thing not telling someone something because you can't, it is quite another, to keep something secret on purpose," she told me.

I wondered if I should have told her about the gun that Heinrich has hidden beneath the floorboards in the barn.

Sergeant Steele looked very stern when he got here. He said they would have to march Heinrich back to the station. We explained that Heinrich has injured his foot and can't walk on it. Sergeant Steele went straight out to the barn and called up to Heinrich.

Heinrich took a while to come down from the loft. When he did, he had his hands in the air and I thought he might tumble but he made it to the bottom.

Sergeant Steele searched him and told him he could put his hands down. Heinrich looked terrified. PC Blake handcuffed him. I don't know why, he wasn't going anywhere. While they decided how they were going to get him to the police station, Heinrich sat on a hay bale and I managed to squeeze next to him.

I held his hand which was difficult with the cuffs but he smiled at me and I swear I almost died. I gave him a hug as best I could and he kissed my cheek. I will remember that moment for the rest of my life.

When the grownups noticed me they got all concerned and told me to go into the house and leave it to them. I didn't of course. I just stood by the door and watched as they gathered Heinrich's things. He didn't have much, there were his boots, which he had to put on, despite his swollen ankle, and his flying jacket. Mummy gave him one of Alfie's old overcoats, the big grey one he used to wear out on the farm. It wouldn't fit Alfie now but it fitted Heinrich. I was glad she did that.

When they weren't paying attention, I managed to get close to him again.

"The gun is still there," he said, nodding towards the hayloft. I didn't know what I was meant to do but there wasn't time to do anything because Sergeant Steele was leaving.

We watched them trudge up the lane until they rounded the bend and were out of sight.

"Well, he will be looked after, I am sure," Mummy decided, pushing me back into the house. I hope that's true. I told Mummy about the gun and she was cross because I hadn't told her before. She said she would deal with it.

I can't stop thinking about Heinrich. Will we ever see him again?

Chapter four

Beatrice

The last line hangs in mid-air it seems. I turn the page but the next is blank. There is nothing to say that the gun was moved nor that Heinrich was ever heard of again. Now I understand why our mother feels some responsibility for Mary's death.

"Grandma must have forgotten," I whisper, my sobs subsiding.

"Yes, she must have," my mother's voice is distant as though she is remembering. I am sad for her now. Grandma Lu would never forgive herself if she knew what had happened but can we in all honesty blame her? Maybe she had looked for the gun and not found it. Maybe my Grandfather and Uncle Alfie had come home and she hadn't wanted them to know she had taken in a young German? So many maybes but none will bring Mary back.

My thoughts take a different turn after that. I am thinking about Hannah's part in all this. If Hannah had not stepped into our world from wherever she came from, would the gun have still fired? Buster might not have been in the barn but the gun could still have fired its fatal bullet. Nicholas may still have dropped it.

For the first time, I don't see Hannah's presence as the single catalyst. Did it all begin with the German airman dropping into our lives, into the lives of our mother? Did it begin long before that? How many events were there to lead to this mess? Can altering just one random event mean that we can change everything? I am beginning to doubt that anything can be changed for the better now. It is all hopeless.

This feeling of helplessness persists for several days. I wish Rachel was here to talk to and mull everything over with but I haven't seen her for a while. I go over events in my mind, again and again, afraid that I might forget something important if I don't.

One afternoon, I make a pact with myself, I will write it all down, just as my mother did. It will be an account of everything and one day, perhaps, it will play an important part in putting things right. One morning, I pick up my diary, filled in with trivia until now, and begin my own story, writing with feverish intent, well into the night, setting down on paper, a nightmare that is all too real right now.

By the time we climb into the car, ready to leave Angel Cottage, for what may well be the last time, I am resigned to a life without my sister. My diary is well hidden. I feel I must leave it at the cottage. Perhaps, if anything happens to me, someone will find it and say,

"So, that's what happened here all that time ago," I chose a good hiding place. There is a loose floorboard behind the chest of drawers in my old room where I used to keep my innermost secrets, locked in an old cash tin. It is the perfect place to hide a diary.

The cottage stands behind us, sad and alone, as we drive away. We have left most of Gran's furniture inside. If Mum and Dad arrange to let it out, they'll need it to be furnished. The new house is modern and small, the furniture we are taking with us, will fill it with ease.

I watch the Devon lanes disappear behind us and imagine what it will be like, to start again, just the four of us.

For three months, I don't give any time to thoughts of Mary, beyond the odd, inescapable memory that forces its way into my head, unasked. With the diary written, I feel released from those thoughts that have dogged my every waking moment for the past few months. I must now try to forget for a bit.

As I throw myself into our new life, it is as though Mary has just gone on a holiday without me. I become adept at avoiding anything that will remind me of her. I have unpacked my things and pushed them into my single chest of drawers. Only my dresses hang in the little wardrobe. There is a bedside table on which I stand Mary's photograph but it is turned to the wall for most of the time. Nicholas is now in his own room. There is just one pink eiderdown in mine. This is a new start, for all of us.

I place my books on the bookshelf that has been built into the alcove. I have not yet opened Mary's suitcase. Mother packed some of her books and favourite dolls in there. She told me I might like to look at them one day. I don't want it. I slide it under the bed and tell myself I will ask Dad to put it in the loft.

My books stand in a neat row on the shelf, their spines familiar and comforting. The line includes Schrödinger's Cat. I ignore it. I eat and sleep and go to school. I don't hear the whispered asides that accompany my entrance to a room full of people who have just become aware of the tragedy that has befallen us. I am successful in blotting everything out, all the bad memories, all the ridiculous ideas I once had, everything locked away in a box in my head.

I would go on like this for longer if I could. I am anaesthetised. Perhaps, if Nicholas had settled down in his new school and we were not the subject of curiosity wherever we went, then maybe, just maybe, I would have been able to forget for longer if not forever. Life is not like that though. We cannot pick and choose what happens to us. Listen to me! What am I saying? That is just what I am proposing to do. I want to choose the outcome of that dreadful afternoon, I want to make it better. Still, as the weeks go by, I think I am coping. I believe that life can be better, we can get over this. I hope that if I get up, go to school, come home, eat, go to bed, often enough, then one day, I will wake up and find that everything is fine. I don't even want to contemplate changing things. This is my life, this is our life, we will just live it.

Some things won't be forgotten though, however hard one tries. One day, about three months after our move to the new house, I find the postcard. The postcard was being used as a bookmark and falls out of the encyclopaedia I am using for my homework. I assume Mary left it there. The postcard belonged to her.

On its own, the postcard is not remarkable. Mary bought it on a day trip to the seaside. She chose it because it carried the image of the doe eyed children she loved. There are three on the card. I remember her picking it up and exclaiming that it was us. The eldest has red hair, the middle one, dark plaits and the youngest, a boy, has holes in his ragged trousers.

"That's you, me and Nick!" she had squealed in delight and bought it to add to her collection. The sentimental tagline reads, "Forget-me-not".

I stare at it for a moment, reading those words and remembering how she laughed.

That is the end of my period of blanking it all out. Forget-me-not. I repeat the words. How could I forget? Tears run free down my face and I cry for the first time it seems, since that day on the stairs when I hid my face in my father's jumper. I don't know if anyone hears me but if they do, they are wise to stay away. I need this time. I need to let it all wash over me. I need to remember.

When the tears have been shed, I stand the postcard on my dressing table, where I can see it. I turn Mary's photograph around so that she smiles at me wherever I go in the room. I vow that I won't forget her. How did I ever think I could? The postcard is like a sign, I think. Mary has sent me a sign.

I remember Rachel and how we both promised to see this thing through to the end.

I can't forget, it is impossible. I don't suppose I ever believed I could. Still, as the weeks continue to go by, I sometimes wonder what it will be like if we do bring Mary back.

Will we forget everything that has happened before? How old will we be? Will we mind, or will we even know to mind? I write to Rachel, a long, rambling letter that attempts to say I have not forgotten, I am still counting on her. I beg a second-class stamp and drop the envelope in the post box on my way to school.

From this point, I am living my life on two levels. On one level, I fit into the family unit as the bereaved sister. I see my parents trying to be so brave as they rebuild their lives. I pretend to be coping and smile and accept my lot. On another level though, I am on a constant lookout for clues. Who is Hannah and where does she come from. Where will she come from? I watch and I wait. I will wait for as long as it takes.

Chapter five

1968

"Mrs Dean? This is Sergeant Phillips, from St Luke's Police Station. We have your son here…Nicholas…."

"Nicholas? Oh no, what has he done now, officer?"

"Been writing graffiti on the toilet wall in the car park. We need you to come and collect him. We've given him a talking to but we realise he has gone through a tough time…we won't take it any further this time."

That is the first time that Nicholas gets into trouble with the police. A week later he has been found fighting in the school playground and they have suspended him for a week. He is then picked up drinking alcohol stolen from the off licence, behind the pavilion.

The misdemeanours are mounting up. The warnings he is receiving are being spent.

On a cold and bleak Thursday morning, we find ourselves waiting for him outside the juvenile court. He is thirteen years old and he and a gang of boys from the estate, have been drinking and creating a disturbance. Something needs to be done about Nicholas.

My parents keep up their constant bickering. I would call it arguing but there is no argument, just a relentless sniping. Neither of them can be bothered to enter into a real argument, perhaps because there isn't anything to argue about. They only seem to agree on one thing, Nicholas will end up in a young offender's prison if he carries on like this.

I take him to one side and ask him what is going on. I know what is going on of course. He has never got over the guilt he feels for Mary's death. He is anxious and depressed though neither emotion is referred to of course. He is labelled as out of control, badly behaved. One day, he might be diagnosed with depression but for now, he is a thirteen-year-old boy who has gone off the rails. It is time to act.

Sitting on the end of his bed, watching while he attacks a crumpet, one I have skived from the kitchen for him, despite him being grounded and confined to his bedroom without supper, I see the little boy who stood in the barn that day. He is now a head taller and his voice is gruff but he is still that same child underneath. I feel his pain because it is also my pain. I share the blame, be that right or wrong.

I watch him for a bit longer before I speak.

"Nick? Remember the girl I saw that Christmas?"

"What girl? Oh, your ghost girl? Yeah, I remember."

"Well, that's the thing, I don't believe she was a ghost, not from the past," I can see he is looking puzzled but I carry on regardless.

"She was too solid, too real— just standing there as solid as you or me, too solid to be a ghost," I say.

"And you have seen a lot of ghosts?" he is mocking me of course.

"No, of course not. It's just that, Rachel and I talked about her a lot when we were staying there and she agrees with me, that girl was no ghost."

"A figment of your imagination then? Considering Rachel didn't even see her that just means you are both nuts," he finishes, swallowing the last of the crumpet, butter dripping down his chin which he swipes away with his sleeve. I ignore this deliberate disgusting behaviour – an action doubtless done for my benefit alone.

"Maybe, but listen, I told her about the Christmas card, the one that vanished, the one from a girl called Hannah. I told her about seeing the girl by the fireplace that day. I couldn't have imagined her twice, maybe more, could I?"

"Don't ask me, you are always making up stories," he shrugs.

"That's different, stories are…stories. This was something else."

"So, if she wasn't a ghost, and let's say you did see something, what are you saying?"

"She came from the future."

The silence is broken by his raucous laughter. I wait until it subsides.

"There's no need to make fun, I know it sounds ridiculous but that girl opened the barn door and let Buster in. She let him in Nick. If she hadn't, Buster wouldn't have knocked the gun out of your hand and…" I stop short, unsure what I am saying now that I have his attention.

"You are one hundred percent mad. For one thing, I probably would have had to drop the gun anyway. It was heavy," his voice trembles a little, "Buster just made it happen sooner, that's all. I killed Mary."

"But that's just it, don't you see? If Buster hadn't been there, you wouldn't have dropped it at that moment. Mary might have moved; lots of things could have changed. Time is everything Nick."

"But how do you know it wouldn't have been you who got shot then? It's ridiculous Bea. I mean, ghost girls and time travellers…"

"Not ridiculous Nick. There is so much that points to it being true," I want to tell him more but I sense he is not going to treat my revelation with any degree of seriousness at the moment, however hard I try. I must be content with having put the idea into his mind. Maybe it will ferment and take root.

"Just tell me this though," I try before I leave him, "Did you make sure the barn door was shut so Buster couldn't get in that day?"

"Ye-es, it was shut. I am sure. The wind almost blew us inside. Don't you remember how strong it was? No way could it have blown open."

"Well, how did Buster get in then?"

I say this as I am walking away. I close the door behind me and take a deep breath. I am hopeful he will think about this for a bit and then be inclined to discuss it further. There is so much more to talk about, so many ways he can help me if only he will believe me. I am tempted to push the subject now but best to leave it be for a while. I am convinced he will want to talk about it again.

I would like to say that our conversation sparks the beginning of an understanding but events don't always go to plan and by evening, Nick is in trouble again. This time it is for stealing from Mum's purse.

"I don't understand why you do it?" Mum is holding her hands up in despair. Nick doesn't even look sorry. He shrugs and carries on eating the apple he picked up on his way to the room to which he has been summoned. Mum is holding her empty purse and demanding where her money has gone. Almost without flinching, Nicholas reaches into his pocket and pulls out three pound notes which he throws on the table.

I suck in my breath. What is happening to my brother?

"Wait until your father gets home…" Mum says at length, retrieving the cash and shaking her head. Her voice is tired and her words a little slurred. Has she been drinking again or is it the tablets she takes like smarties, dulling her speech? It is hard to tell. As for waiting for our father to get home. We could have a long wait. Dad stays longer at the office thcse days and if I am honest, he appears to try to avoid coming home at all.

Nicholas's punishment is swift, once Dad hears about his theft. A clip around the ear and my brother emerges red faced from the dining room. Dad's face is grim when I next see him. I don't say anything because there are no excuses for what Nick did.

"It's as though he wants us to punish him," Dad sighs when Mum comes into the room. I think he is right. Nick feels so guilty, he wants to be punished and will continue to misbehave until he feels he has received the correct punishment for the crime, the crime of killing his sister. The realisation hurts and I retire to my bedroom to think.

Schrödinger's Cat is squashed between The Canterbury Tales and The Chalet School Stories. I pull it off the shelf with trembling fingers and open it at the page Rachel and I pored over for so long. I take a deep breath and read. Once again, it is a perfect fit with what I know to be true. I am not imagining it. We can change things. I know we can and we must.

Chapter six
1973

It has been eleven years since Mary's death. She would be almost twenty-four now, had she lived. Where would she be? Where would any of us be now if she had not died? I graduated with an English degree last year and shunning teaching or any job that might take me too far from Lanscott, I have been working in the local library ever since. I met Ray in my second year of University and we have been seeing each other for the same amount of time. He knows about my past. He knows about Nick and he has met my parents so he is all too aware of how things are with them. I have not told him about Rachel and me, how we hope to change things. I would like to confide in him but the older I get, the harder it becomes to justify changing anything. At this rate, I will be fighting just to keep things the same. It is ironic really.

I still like to write. I love to write the stories that run through my mind but the greatest story I could write, which would not be fiction at all, has yet to be finished. Ironically, if the story reaches it preferred conclusion, then there will be no story to tell. I wrestle with this concept almost daily.

"When is a story not a story?" What is the punch line? Your guess is as good as mine.

Nicholas greeted the lowering of the coming of age to 18, with glee, using it as an excuse to put two fingers up to the world and go his own way as soon as he could. Having shirked college, he was adamant he was not going to go to university. He just upped and left the day after his eighteenth birthday. To be fair, it must have been hard being at home on his own with our parents while I was away at University. God knows, going home for the weekend was always something of a chore for me. To my amazement, our parents are still together, in name at least. Our mother drinks too much and eats too little. Our father spends most of his time at work or at the golf club, but he is at least, still living at home.

I don't know if my mother is relieved that Nicholas has left home or feels guilty for the way his life has turned out. We all know that guilt plagued him all those years and now he has to find a way to survive.

Nicholas and I have never spoken about that conversation we had when he was thirteen, not once, since. If he did think about what I said, it has never been evident to me.

There was a brief time, when I first left university, that I tried living under the same roof as my parents again but after three stressful weeks, during which I put up with their prolonged cold silences and forced smiles, I knew I had to find my own place. Ray's offer came at just the right time. This small flat we find ourselves in, is far from luxury but it is comfortable and here I can pretend for a while that everything is fine. The days can come and go without any need to think about the past. For a short time, I am cocooned in the new and the wonderful. We are almost ridiculously happy. Ray and I enjoy our new domesticity and I begin to believe I could be happy living this way, even if nothing ever changed. Despite this, I keep the postcard close. Forget-me-not.

When a break through does come, it is from an unexpected source. Despite Nicholas's reluctance to remain in contact with our parents, he does keep in contact with me and despite not appearing to believe in or even acknowledge what we spoke about all those years ago, he has sent me something that puts a whole new spin on things. It is a photograph taken with the box brownie that we used on that terrible afternoon in the barn. It must have had some film in it after all.

Ray is at work. The library is closed today and I have been pottering around our little flat, considering painting the kitchen. When the letter falls on the mat, I recognise the handwriting straight away. Why would Nicholas be writing to me? The message is short and to the point.

"Look and take your time, is this your ghost girl?"
I pull the photograph out of its sleeve and stare, moving the desk lamp towards me in order to study it. Nicholas has had it blown up to a reasonable size.

The black and white print lies on the table. I find myself dropping into the nearest chair.
Mary must have taken this, I reason. Here am I, strutting my stuff in a poncho, and there she is, unseen behind the camera, identified only by her shadow. I wish for a moment I had taken the camera from her and snapped her instead. Then I see the girl. In the far recesses of the picture, there is a definite shape behind me, her face highlighted by the single bulb. She looks startled as though she has only just realised where she is. Her features are a little blurred but the clothes, the hair, they belong to her. My breath seems to leave my body.
She was there!

I sit here, staring at the image for some time. I want to bring it into focus but the blurry Kodochrome is all I have. It is more than I have ever had before. I trace the outline with a trembling finger. My Ghost Girl, except she wasn't, was she? Whoever heard of a ghost being in a photograph, unless superimposed? The girl is wearing trousers, some sort of plimsoll on her feet and her top is emblazoned with a slogan that is impossible to read. Her hair hangs loose around her shoulders. The black and white film suggests it is fair. I remember then, the memory jogged by this gem of a find, I remember her face, her snub nose, there was a slogan on her yellow jumper, I remember now. The five Olympic rings above the word, London. It must be a clue, it has to be.

I tuck the photograph into its wallet and place it in the drawer of my desk. I want to call Nicholas but I know he doesn't have a phone. I will need to go and see him. The fact that he sent me this, suggests he did take notice of what I said all those years ago and I am curious to know how he came by the photograph and if there are any more where it came from.

His flat is cold, perched on the second floor of a dark, dank building off the Waterloo road, it has no view to speak of and mould spreads it fingers across the walls. A cold draught encircles my ankles where I sit. Still, I can see he has tried to make it home. An old armchair that I recognise as the one our parents used to have in their study, sits in one corner. There are other echoes of our past, a picture on the wall I remember Grandma Lu having, a game of monopoly on the coffee table (who does he play with?) so he hasn't disowned all of it then. He ushers me in without a word and disappears to make a pot of tea. I take the opportunity to appraise my surroundings.

"Like it? A bit minimalist, don't you think?" I laugh,

"It isn't as bad as I had imagined as it happens."

"Well, the chair arrived last week. Dad was sorting through some stuff and asked if I wanted it." I am surprised,

"Have you seen him?"

"We meet up now and then,"

I am surprised. I had thought he had broken all ties with our parents. It is evident that he has not.

"And before you ask, no, I have not seen mother. Dad says she is pretty much out of it most of the time."

102

I bite my lip, yes, it is true. Our mother has never recovered from Mary's death and blaming herself, much as Nicholas has done, she has turned to the bottle and tranquilizers for solace. I only see her when I have to. The experience is too distressing to repeat too often.

"They've split up you know," he drops that piece of news into the conversation as he hands me a mug of tea. I look up sharply. I have always thought they would but to hear it, that's something else.

"When?"

"Last month. Oh, Mother wouldn't have told you, if she even knows that is. Dad says he just got tired of being lonely. Mother doesn't speak to anyone these days," he puts his own mug on the coffee table and stares at it for a moment, "It's so sad," he says.

We sit in silence for a moment, drinking tea and nibbling on ginger snaps which he has managed to rustle up from somewhere.

"The photograph?" I question after a suitable pause, "Where did you get it?"

"Rachel,"

"Rachel?" I am incredulous. I haven't seen Rachel for ages, not since the baby was born and Gemma must be over a year old by now. I had no idea she was in touch with Nick.

"Yes, she was there when, well, Aunt Jean went over to make sure Mother was all right with Dad gone and Rachel was helping her sort a few things out. Must have been one of Mother's rare lucid moments. She asked them to take a box of rubbish to the tip and this," he reached round and pulled the old box brownie out of a box in the corner,

"Luckily, Rachel spotted this inside and decided it shouldn't be thrown away," he strokes the reddish-brown box with something approaching reverence. She decided to take it home and that's when she realised there was still a film inside,"

"Something we didn't know," I interject.

"Quite, well, she managed to get the film developed. It was in pretty bad shape, the film – not much could be saved I mean but what was amazing is, the one I sent you, that was a copy of course, that was among them."

"There were others then?"

"Only a couple of all of us on the beach that summer. It was this one that rang alarm bells though, the one with the girl in the background. I'm sorry, Bea, I never did believe you but this was taken that day wasn't it? Christmas Eve? It must have been the last one on the reel. None of the others you pretended to snap came out. But this one, it shows that girl, the one you kept saying you saw," he stops.

I stare at him. So, he has never really, believed me, not truly, not for a second, until this chance find…but was it chance? There seems to be something meant, about all this. If truth is to be told, I am relieved that I have not dreamt it because I have wondered over the years. The surety of a child gave way to the distrust of youth and after University it all seemed so ridiculous and unlikely.

I pull the photograph out of my bag and lay it on the table.

"What does it mean?" I ask, tentative now that we have this new understanding. He shrugs.

"You tell me Bea. She was there, she doesn't look like a regular ghost. So, did she really influence anything or would it all have happened just the way it did with or without her? I just can't get my head around it to be honest, but I am trying…"
I swallow hard.

"What did Rachel say?" I can't believe Rachel confided this in Nicholas and not me but then she doesn't even know where I am living these days. She'd have got Nick's address through Dad. I feel a stab of guilt at not having kept in touch as I had planned. A picture of two young girls, swearing to get to the bottom of this tragedy, flits before my eyes. Well, Rachel has kept her part of the bargain, that's for sure.

"She just turned up here with the photo and asked me about you, what you are up to, where you are living etc. She said I must send you the photo and then we can all meet up."

"Meet up?" I look around, half expecting to see Rachel walk into the room here and now.

"She's in Scotland at the moment," he grins, "Tom is teaching up there for a bit I think,"
I nod, thoughtful now,

"So, what do we do?" I am thinking aloud. Nicholas does not reply for a while. At long last, he stands up,

"I think we will have something stronger," he decides.

I must say I am open to the idea, my head is spinning with all this new information and nothing is clear, despite me thinking how this photo is so important. After all, we see the girl but I have seen her before, how do I know where she has come from, when she came and whether or not I can warn her somehow. Nicholas shares my concerns but unlike me, he has had longer to think about it. He has done some research.

"Look at this," he says, passing me another version of the print. This one has been blown up even more. The slogan on the girl's top flies into focus. The five Olympic rings sit on top of the word London which, now that I can see it enlarged, is written in such a way that the first part seems also to say 2012.

I mouth the date, 2012. What does it mean?

"It's a date, don't you see? I assume that in 2012 the Olympic Games will come to London. Now that'd be a coup eh? Don't suppose we could put a bet on? What do you think?"

I am sceptical. The Olympics, London – not necessarily, I think. It seems certain though, the jumper was issued for the Olympic Games. I think back, the last time we hosted the games was 1948. This was before I was born. 2012 is so far away, I am a little disappointed. Do we have to wait until 2012 for our ghost girl to appear?

"But that's ages away Nick," I do a mental calculation, I will be in my sixties!" the notion is strange. Here I am, in my twenties, contemplating waiting a further forty years before I can begin to put right this tragedy that has been our life. Will it be worth the wait? Can it possibly justify all we have gone through?

"I think we need to discuss what we do from here, Bea."

"What do you mean? What can we do?"

"Well, that's just it, we don't have to do anything. We know the girl was there and we know that things might have been different if she hadn't been, but, as for changing what happened, well, do we want to?"

I am confused, is this not what we have always dreamt of being able to do?

"Yes, but think, Bea. Suppose we wait until 2012 and we find this girl, suppose, just suppose, we can use physical force to stop her going into the barn on Christmas Eve. How do we know that if Mary didn't get shot, then one of us would not have died instead? Suppose the girl didn't have anything to do with it even, suppose she was just watching. Buster could have got in another way, a hole in the barn wall, nothing to do with her. We'd wait all that time, not living our lives properly and for what?"

"Living our lives properly? Isn't that what we have been doing?" I know, before he answers that he sees his life in other ways.

"Not me, Bea. I have been hiding. What happened was an accident, bloody awful, tragic accident. I have come to terms with that now. I've seen people, had therapy," he looks sheepish at the admission, "I had to, I needed to stop what was happening to me. I missed out on college, but I might get some qualifications, turn my life around. I guess I am saying, what will be, will be."

I look down at the photograph again,

"That's good Nick, honestly, I am pleased for you but I have to try and find her, you know that don't you?"
He nods and passes me a glass of wine.

"I know, just saying," he shrugs, "I have no problem with you looking but don't put your life on hold Bea, that's all I ask."

"I won't," I tell him, tucking the photographs into my bag.

"If you aren't sure, why did you send me the photograph? Why not keep quiet?" I am curious now.

"How on earth could I do that? Apart from the fact that I promised Rachel I would tell you about it, part of me wants to find her too,"

I am relieved. I share his reservations too. I have so many doubts and concerns about this entire thing that it scares me sometimes but I also know we have to find the girl, whatever we do after that, will be up to us. Maybe we will choose to do nothing.

"You still seeing that chap, the one you were with at Uni?"
I think of Ray, waiting for me back at the flat. Of course, we are still together, didn't he ask me to marry him just last week? I don't confide this last to Nick but he has made me think. I won't put my life on hold but neither will I stop looking. I can't.

Rachel is more excited about events than Nicholas appeared to be. She calls me the next day.

"Oh, you know Nick, he just wants to wait and see what happens but there's no harm in following this up is there? Two pairs of eyes and ears are better than one, eh Bea?" I love Rachel, she won't be beaten.

"I suppose so, there isn't much we can do, at the moment, except wait but we can plan what we will do, when we find her," I suggest. Rachel is ecstatic,

"Let's meet up," she enthuses.

We get together a week later at the library where I am working. It seems a good place to sit and catch up and a good place to think without interruptions. Rachel has left Gemma with her mother. I ask how her husband is, how the teaching is going, she tells me about Gemma's latest achievements, I tell her about Ray and our very new engagement and then, when all the pleasantries are out of the way, we sit back and stare at each other. We haven't had a chance to catch up since Gemma was born, two years ago. There is so much to say.

Rachel has come equipped with a scrapbook. She has a copy of the photograph and a detailed description of events leading up to Mary's death, including newspaper cuttings from the time. She watches my face in case seeing it all laid out like that, should upset me but I am hardened against such things by now.

The newspapers were less than kind in some reports. One blamed our parents for allowing the gun to remain undetected all those years (what could they have done differently?) another wondered if we had been allowed to run riot and cited a lack of discipline as the probable main root cause of the accident. One reported that Nicholas had been a strange, quiet boy which was not true at all, yet another described Mary as wilful and wild. I was struck by the total lack of sympathy they showed toward our grieving parents. A week later, the story had died from all but the local press, where it occupied a spot below the placing of a new waste bin in the park. It said simply,

"Tragic family grieve the loss of their daughter," with a grainy photograph of us walking in the park. I don't remember the incident.

"The Olympic rings, that must be a clue, the biggest yet. I am amazed you didn't mention that before Bea," she says, her fingers pointing to the girl in the photograph.

"I didn't remember until I saw the photo, to be honest," I tell her.

She smiles and draws a quick sketch of the sweatshirt with its slogan.

"The word London, reads as 2012 too, it's quite a clever use of fonts," I murmur.

She agrees and writes the date next to the sweatshirt.

She pats the next empty page, "this is where we start, recording anything and everything that we find to do with the girl. It's a shame we don't have the Christmas card you know."

I had forgotten about the Christmas card, the glittery snow scene depicting traditional cottage and fields. I had forgotten about the words I read, "With love from Hannah,"

"It doesn't matter, it was just a card, it's what was in it that matters and I do remember that," I tell her. We take another page and write the details on it.

"There will be more, I am sure of it," Rachel promises. I believe her.

"There is one more thing to go in here now though, the Cat book, Schrödinger's Cat. I think it's important."
I am surprised she has remembered the book. I have thought of little else since the photo turned up.

"I still have that copy," I tell her and watch her eyes light up. "There is also one in the Quantum Theory section here, I'll get it," I go straight to it.

Together, we re-read the book, turning the pages one by one.

When we have finished, we exchange understanding glances. For a moment we could be twelve again, huddling beneath an eiderdown.

We write the title and the summary of the book on the page beneath the Christmas card details. Something can be deemed not to have happened until it is seen to happen. The barn becomes the box, the cat is Mary and the gun the poisonous substance. For as long as no one looks inside, Mary can be both alive and dead. I am so happy that Rachel conceives the concept and does not think me a total lunatic. Schrodinger has no idea how he has helped me. How surprised would he be to learn that his spoof theory might work, for us at least?

I pause as Rachel underlines the words.

"Nick is worried about how things will change," I tell her, "If we stop what happened, happening. What do you think? Do you think it is wrong to try to change things?" Rachel ponders the question for a while, chewing her lip just as she used to as a child. Mary did that too. I am moved by the sight.

"I think we owe it to ourselves and to Mary, to try. Just think, what would your life have been like if Mary had lived?"

The question is loaded. What indeed? I don't believe I would be doing anything different. Nicholas, however, is a different matter. He may have had a less rocky path and our parents, they used to be so happy or was that just a child's view? Were the cracks already there? Would they have drifted apart anyway? There is no way of knowing.

The notion of one of us being shot instead still hangs there, unspoken. What is meant to be will be. If I was meant to do nothing would I have seen the girl and would Rachel have found the photograph? I can no more stop trying to find this girl from the future than I can stop breathing.

"Would you like to keep this?" Rachel is pushing the scrapbook towards me. I thank her but she should have it. In case anything happens to me. I want her to carry on if that happens. She is grateful. I have my memory of that afternoon. I no longer want to bury it. I want to remember every second. I need to remember because that is the only way I will find out how to stop the accident happening again.

I don't give a thought to what might happen to the girl in the Photograph afterwards. Not now. It will be a very long time before I have any misgivings about finding her and by then it will be too late. Now, I walk Rachel to the train station and wave her away with hope in my heart. I go back to my flat where I down the last of the wine and read Schrödinger's Cat once again.

It is almost 1974. Where will Hannah be born? Who are her parents going to be? In 38 years' time, she will be about twelve, I guess. Maybe thirteen. A baby born in 2000 perhaps. Born to parents who themselves, have not yet been born. I try to imagine that fact. Hannah's parents may not yet be alive. I spend the evening jotting down possibilities. It seems to me that if Hannah was staying at the cottage at Christmas time, exploring as she was, she would have been staying there for a short time, not living. My parents have never given any indication of wanting to sell the cottage and it has been let out over the past few summers, to holidaymakers who hanker after cream teas and green fields. I must continue to monitor who stays there and one day, she will come. I am sure of it because in my world, it has already happened.

There is a niggle at the back of my mind of course. Perhaps I will die of natural causes before she appears, perhaps the cottage will be sold or be burnt down, yet, despite these slight misgivings, I am resolute. It will happen.

The one thing I do not think of that evening, but which comes to me in the middle of the night and come to think of it, is the very thing I should be looking at, is how she gets through time in the first place. Is there a tunnel? A window? A fissure in time? I cannot rule anything out. I go back to sleep dreaming of time warps and shattering glass.

Somewhere between the witching hour and the first cock crow, I feel my heart begin to thud. My eyes snap open. What have I heard? Beside me, Ray snores gently. We have been married for a total of one month. It is a moment before I realise it is not a sound that has woken me but a realisation.

Lying there, in the darkness of the room, I am seeing the kitchen, just as it was that Christmas. The table, the mugs of Cocoa, the cherubs sitting on the mantelpiece, the Angel clock with its strange, double ticking hands. Double ticking? Yes, I hear them now, Dad is adjusting the mechanism as he does every night because once in each twenty-four-hour period, the clock ticks over the hour with a double tick so that after several days it is running fast.

I lie there, remembering how he would twist the hands back and tap the glass to ensure the clock continued its sojourn. The cherubs would stare down benignly but as I revisit that scene, a scene replayed so many times over the years, I am struck by the certain knowledge that it was the clock that enabled Hannah to cross into our time, a quirk of time, created as the clock played Russian roulette with our lives.

I am seized with a desire to pull it from the wall and smash it but even if I could, it is too late for that. If Hannah

112

does not use the opportunity to try and change what happened, then things may stay as they are. There is no guarantee that by removing Hannah from the scene, that Buster won't get in and cause the same accident to take place. I need her to be there but I need her to be forewarned. How can that happen?

There is only one sure way, if I can be sure of anything. The clock must play on and events must unfold. I wonder, as I slip into a more restful sleep, whether anyone has been adjusting the clock in our absence. Would anyone notice? By now it must be running very fast if not. Doubtless, someone will turn the hands back to their correct time. Perhaps Dad adjusts it each time he goes back to check on things. Will this matter? I doubt it. I have a feeling though the clock is the vital link that will bring Hannah to us back in 1963.

Maybe I will destroy it afterwards, just in case. As the thoughts play out in my head, sleep claims me and I think no more.

1975

Rachel and I are going to sit by the river, feed the ducks and think of good things. It is late Autumn but a mild Autumn this year. Rachel is heavily pregnant again. She lumbers along the tow path pushing Gemma in her buggy.

Gemma is three years old. She is a mini carbon copy of her father having his jet black curls and sparkling blue eyes. Rachel has declared more than once that she thinks it unfair a child she has carried for nine months and given birth to, should fail to resemble her in the slightest and go out of her way to be her exact opposite in all things. I hope the next one will be kinder to her and inherit some of her fair, delicate looks. Gemma begins shouting at the ducks and flapping her arms in excitement. Rachel grimaces as she settles on the seat next to me.

"Aren't you going to let her out?" I tease.

"In a minute, must catch my breath first…if I let her out she will run riot and, in all probability, terrorise the poor ducks," she confides. I laugh. Gemma is a live wire but hardly a monster. I undo her strap and sit her on my knee from where she gabbles about the ducks and the bread we are feeding them and is no trouble at all.

"Hmm, for you she is like that. For me? You don't want to know," Rachel sighs, shading her eyes against the low sun.

We give the ducks names and Gemma breaks the bread into edible chunks. After 10 minutes, she demands to slide off my lap and take me to see the iron frog that sits on the wall next to us.

"She loves you, Bea," Rachel grins, "She's always so well behaved for you too. Must be your natural authoritative nature – Mary always said you should be a teacher the way you ordered us around."
Mention of Mary makes me smile too.

These days, I don't think of Mary every minute of the day. Truth to tell, I might go days without giving her more than a passing thought. You can't grieve forever and it has been almost twenty years now.

Sitting here, with Gemma and a very pregnant Rachel, I can't help wondering whether I would have been an auntie by now, a real auntie that is. Gemma calls me auntie but I am her second cousin. Nicholas seems to display no intentions of settling down, preferring to play the field and spend his money on travelling by all accounts. Since the discovery of the photo and our frank discussion, I have seen little of him. He has taken himself off to some far-flung corner of the earth. He has gone to find himself, he told me in a postcard from Istanbul. Nicholas is still the bane of my life. My parents don't understand why he has gone away just as he appeared to be sorting himself out.

They are still living apart but when it comes to telling us what they think, they seem to join forces again. I am not convinced they want to be apart at all. Whatever they feel about their son, I will not give up on him.

"Something wrong?" My attention is grabbed by Rachel's sudden groan.

"No, no, I am fine, just a twinge I think…"

"Well, maybe we should get you back to your mum's?"

We are both staying with Rachel's mum while Tom is working away. The baby is due any day. I have volunteered to watch Gemma when Rachel goes into labour – shunning a home birth she has opted for a stay at the cottage hospital so she can rest. Ray just shrugged and laughed when I told him I was staying for a while. He always says Rachel and I are thick as thieves and doesn't know what we find to talk about half the time. I do not enlighten him.

Back at Aunt Jean's, we release Gemma and watch her career through the hall and into the dining room. Aunt Jean fusses around Rachel and suggests we go into the conservatory where she will bring us a cup of tea and some home-made biscuits. It is a tempting idea but one that never quite makes it to fruition. As we take off our coats, Rachel doubles over and with a rueful nod, tells us that this is it. Aunt Jean pulls on her coat, picks up the bag that has been sitting, packed, in the hallway for weeks, and bundles Rachel out to the car.

"I'll phone you when I know what's happening, Bea," she calls.

I wave at them from the door, "Well, we know what's happening, don't we Gem?" I smile, picking the girl up and letting her wave goodbye to her mummy and grandma. Though I am not at all sure Gemma understands that she is about to become a big sister.

"Right then, Gem, what now?" I say, as the car shoots off into the distance.

I stare at her for a moment, she is clutching a ball of wool that is half unravelled. A long forgotten memory comes to mind, of Mary unpicking a jumper that Grandma Lu had given her and winding the wool into a ball so it could be reknitted into something new. We unpicked a lot of jumpers in those days and reused the wool. It is just what one did. For a moment, I imagine that it is Mary and I who are staying at Aunt Jean's. My sister would be in her mid-twenties now, would she have finished her training and be a fully-fledged Doctor? Would she have married and maybe have children who would be playing with Gemma, even now?

I think of Rachel, always so adamant we must find that girl from the future. Preposterous though the theory is, I do still believe, I think. I still hope at least. I can do nothing but hope since finding the photograph. Now we even have a clue as to when, if not where, we will find her. The where, I presume is not relevant as the only thing that matters, is that she is at the cottage on Christmas Eve and I presume she achieves that without any help from me.

I go over to Gemma and suggest we make some cookies for when Mummy gets home. She is jumping up and down at the thought and I resign myself to a very messy afternoon.

The cookies are sitting cooling on the side and Gemma is bathed and ready for bed by the time the phone rings.

"Oh Bea, it's another girl!" Aunt Jean's voice cracks with emotion and it takes me a while to get any more from her.

"It's a girl, you have another niece," I tell Nicholas, when I do manage to get hold of him. He still doesn't have a phone of his own but I leave several messages with his landlady in London with whom he checks back for messages every so often. He is back in the country it transpires. He has been somewhere in Birmingham at an exhibition. The minute he can, he phones me from the nearest payphone. I tell him that Mother and baby are doing well and Tom made it to the hospital in time for the birth. If all goes well, they will be home in a few days.

"Excellent! What have they called her?" he asks, his interest genuine.

"I don't know. No one has told me. I am not sure they have even chosen a name yet. I think they both thought this one would be a boy. Are you coming down to see us?" I ask, after the pips have gone for the second time and he has fed yet more money into the pay phone.

"Not sure, I'll try, funds are a bit tight right now," he hedges. I won't hold my breath. I haven't seen Nicholas since that day in his flat when we found the photograph. All the things I would like to discuss with him, will have to wait because I must respect his reluctance to commit fully to this dubious search. It would be nice to see him though.

"Well, I am planning to take Gemma up to the hospital tomorrow to meet the new arrival…"

"Oh, I won't go to the hospital…sorry Bea but, well, you know…"

I know. Nicholas's phobia of hospitals can doubtless be traced to the trauma of spending so much time there that dreadful Christmas Eve. I don't press him on the subject. Rachel is home by the weekend. I see them settled in before making a tactful retreat. Aunt Jean can now take charge of Gemma.

"What are you calling her?" I remember to ask, before I go.

"Rebecca Mary," says Rachel and I feel a lump form in my throat. Rebecca. It is a pretty name and Mary, of course. It makes perfect sense.

"Lovely," I say.

"We thought about calling her Mary Rebecca but I said you might want to use that name, when the time comes," I laugh, Ray and I do not plan on having children but I don't say this to Rachel. She will only read into it more than there is to see.

To say I see a lot of Rachel and the children from that day would not be true. Our paths cross at intervals over the years, at birthdays and Christmas get togethers and the odd funeral, but, on the whole, life overtakes us and we find ourselves communicating by phone more than face to face. We no longer live near enough to one another to allow us to call in on a whim.

Nicholas manages to hold down a job for more than a couple of months and is put in charge of "Goods Out" at a mail order company. At long last, he seems to have settled down although he still keeps his distance from family. When we do meet up, on most occasions because I have arranged everything and all but bullied him into it, he seems happy enough.

We don't discuss what happened all those years ago any more. You can't put your life on hold for an indefinite time, that much I have learnt. You have to live for today, too. Besides, we are all getting older now.

Chapter seven

"They say it is inoperable,"
I stare at my cousin, still not comprehending this news she has just confided. Tom looks no different to me, striding across the garden, spade in hand. We are sitting in Rachel's conservatory in late September.

"But there must be something…"
She shakes her head.

"No, Bea. They have tried everything, the way the tumour is lying…and he has smoked all his life," she bites her lip and I reach out to grab her hand. This cannot be true. How can a man like Tom, so full of life, so vibrant, be about to die?

"How long have they said?" I use the word 'they' as though I might know these faceless people who have made this pronouncement.
Rachel shakes her head, her voice breaking a little,

"Three months, six…"
Tom waves at me as he winds in the garden hose, I wave back.

"But, he looks…"

"So well? Yes, that's what I said. It's a blessing, they told me, but it won't last. He will go downhill and then…"

It is a hard thing to hear but even harder for Rachel to impart. I am angry that she should be going through this and for once, my own preoccupation with changing the past is forgotten. Indeed, it now seems obscene to want to change anything. How could I be so arrogant as to think we could? How fair would it be?

"Do the girls know?" I know that Gemma is on a Gap Year somewhere in Australia and Becky has just started seeing someone called George. Neither girls live at home. She nods.

"They are devastated. Gemma is coming home as soon as she can get a flight and Becky has offered to move back in, to help me. I have told her not to of course,"

I wonder how Rachel will cope. I wonder how I will cope. This is a selfish thought and not one I am proud of. I have leant on Rachel too much in my life. I will push these selfish thoughts of changing things to suit me, to one side and I will give my cousin all the support she needs. I make this resolution as we wash the dishes after dinner. Tom has gone back into the garden to water the lawn.

No one mentions the subject of his illness throughout dinner. Rachel has already told me Tom would rather it that way. I can understand that. For my part, seeing him appearing so well, is disarming.

"He just looks so, full of life," my words sound lame when I tell Ray later. Ray sighs. He and Tom, though never bosom buddies, have always got along well.

"Tom's a good sort," he tells me.

For once, I don't think much about Mary and the accident that Christmas. Rachel, Tom and the girls, are spending a quiet Christmas at home. Jean, herself widowed some years ago, has gone over to be with them but there is no big family get together, no fuss. Tom knows it may be his last.

Ray and I invite Nicholas, as we always do, but he is somewhere in Nepal and promises to call in, in the New year. We make the obligatory visit to Mum and Dad's house where an uneasy peace has descended of late, Dad having moved back some time at the end of June, but on the whole, Christmas 1995 is a sombre and somewhat lonesome affair. We don't even go back to the cottage, something I have insisted on doing every year since we met.

By February, Tom is showing signs of deteriorating. With his hair, now grey and thinning, his eyes, sunken in his head, he no longer resembles the vibrant character we know. He is very positive though. He tells us he is not in any real pain and he is lucky to have had so much time with his beautiful wife and daughters. He talks about death as though it is just like going into the next room, without us. I am struck by how calm he is when talking about it. I am also aware that I share his feelings about death. How do I cope with all this and still keep the image of Mary alive in my mind, the image of a living Mary? I don't know, but I do.

Gemma cut short her travels and has been staying with her parents for the past few weeks, as has Rebecca, though the latter's stay may be short lived if Rachel doesn't reign in her comments about her new boyfriend, I fear. Rebecca has started seeing George Robinson, much to Rachel's displeasure. Rachel tells me Rebecca is infatuated. I am not quite sure why she disapproves so much of this liaison but when I mention it to her she confides that George Robinson is not only several years older than Rebecca but he is also divorced. His family are Rag and Bone men and he is a travelling salesman. I have to smile at the final revelation.

"But he isn't that much older, Rachel. Seven years is nothing," I say, trying not to smile. Rachel is so very forgiving as a rule but she has a bee in her bonnet, that's for sure,

"Seven years is a lot when Becky is only 20 and his parents gazumped us on our first house as well. As for being a travelling salesman, well, goodness knows what he gets up to."

I stifle a laugh and receive a withering look in return,

"You don't understand, not having children," she says, a tad more spite in her words than she means I think. I forgive her, she is under a lot of stress.

"What does Tom think?" I venture, after a moment.

"Oh, he thinks the sun shines out of the boy's backside," she says.

I don't say anything, I just stare at her. We both know Tom has always been a very good judge of character.

"All right, all right, I admit it, he is nice enough but seven years…her voice breaks, I don't want Becky to go through what we are going through…an older husband…being widowed…"

I see at once where she is coming from. There is a five-year age gap between her and Tom. I understand. It may not be the most logical of reasons but it makes more sense to me now. I don't let the jibe about me being childless get to me. We didn't set out not to have children, it just never happened. Neither of us have been worried by it. If I am to be honest with myself, I have never thought it a good idea, given my preoccupation with change.

I smile at my cousin who is looking a little sheepish now,

"I think, you have to just let your children do what they want to do," I tell her.

I have met George only a couple of times but he seems a decent chap and it is obvious he is besotted with Rebecca. I feel sorry for the pair of them, facing such opposition. I do my best to assist by fighting his cause with Rachel. Tom says little. Rachel is worried about Tom I know. Her worry over Tom soon stops her fretting about Rebecca's relationship with George Robinson. She is soon caught up in hospital visits and it is not long before the inevitable happens.

By the time August comes around, Tom has slipped away. George proves himself to be invaluable in sorting things out for her after the funeral. He and Becky make sure she needs for nothing. Rachel forgets she ever had any objections to their relationship. She tells everyone who will listen, what a great couple they make.

Rebecca and George marry early in 1996. The Olympic games will be held in Atlanta this year and in 2000, Sydney, Australia. Ray and I are at the wedding and Rachel and I do manage to catch up again for a bit, with a few tears of course, because Tom cannot be here to see his youngest daughter get married but it is a happy occasion, nonetheless and she hides her sadness well. By this time, I am in my late forties. Rebecca and George find a small house quite close to Rachel. Joe is born a year later. I pop in with a card and a blue romper suit. Apart from that brief meeting, Joe and I don't meet again until he is almost three.

By this time, I have lived more than three decades longer than Mary. Despite this, I will not believe that fate decreed she should die. Still, when everyone thinks I have given up, I look for that little girl who could provide the key.

Although we have the year that she may have come from, I am aware that this may be a red herring as far as timing goes. Suppose she is wearing an old sweater, one from much later? Suppose the year means nothing at all? I could live and die before she ever steps through that time portal. What then? History would be recorded the same as it is today. Nothing would change. Is that so bad a thing? I have to ask myself the question because my life is pretty good.

The thought of things remaining the same, is not as abhorrent to me as I would have once thought and I feel guilty about that, an emotion that is not quite rational. Age brings with it contentment on certain levels. We grow used to ourselves and we become comfortable within our lives. I cannot, in all honesty, say I am unhappy in the life we have

123

led. Our parents are now growing frail and cause us all sorts of problems but they seem to have come to terms with things and although they no longer share a bedroom, they do spend a lot of time in each other's company. They are reluctant companions I suppose and grief has been tucked away, lest it disrupt this tenuous link again. Who is to say they should not be like this? With my thoughts going down this path, it would be easy to just let things lie now, easy yes, but I would feel I am betraying the child I once was if I do not keep looking. That said, it occurs to me now, if I do nothing, how will the young girl react to seeing such a terrible accident? Will it not traumatise her? Will she think she has imagined everything? I have not thought about her in this way before but now I feel I must do something to protect her, as well. What I will be able to do if I manage to find the girl, is as yet undecided.

As the years go by, I feel sure we are getting close. I tell myself I will not look beyond 2012 though. If she does not appear then, I shall admit defeat. All our suppositions, our beliefs will be held up to question. The photograph is still in my drawer. I don't look at it often. I don't need to. Its image is embedded on my brain. The photograph is the biggest clue to when she will appear, that we have. Indeed, it is the only clue come to think of it.

As time goes by I can see fashions change but trends come and go. The girl's outfit could have come from anywhere in the recent past or the future, but for the date embedded in the motif. Therein lies the real clue. I listen to each announcement of where the next Olympic Games will be held with bated breath. I know I don't have too much longer to wait and it becomes imperative that Rachel and I get together, Nicholas too if I can persuade him. I have not confided in Johnny and I don't think Rachel ever has, either. In my heart, I am convinced that 2012 is the year in which Hannah will travel back to 1963 and can prevent what happened then from happening.

It is a lot to hang my hat on, I know, but I do. I have told no one except Rachel and Nicholas. What would be the point? Anyone else would think me mad. They already think I was strange as a child, those who remember me, with my talk of ghosts and the like. Rachel alone believes in this as much, if not more so, than I.

I feel the urge to contact her again but life has other ideas. We head in opposite directions for a while. Gemma invites Rachel to join them in America for a long holiday while she follows a research project in Florida for six months and I find myself caught up in a shift in library politics. The library I was working in is due to close and we are working hard to reverse the decision. It takes the better part of a year before I realise it is a forlorn hope and I must look for another position. It is ironic that I find one close to my childhood home. The library in the nearest town appoints me as head librarian and we move to a cottage in a village a stone's throw from Angel Cottage.

Events move quite fast but still, it is two full years until I see Rachel again. She is now back in England and eager to meet up. She is more than delighted to find that I am living in the area again and we make a date to get together.

The day we arrange to meet, it is hot and sultry. There is a feeling of malaise amongst the holidaymakers strolling the streets. I am wearing a wide brimmed hat and perspiration collects on my brow. I see Rachel, before she sees me. She is brushing a wasp away and her attention is taken for a moment.

I grin and wave at her as I cross the road. She looks flushed, maybe it is the wasp, maybe it is the heat. Seeing me, she squeals in delight and we hug before heading off to the welcome cool of the coffee shop. Once settled with coffee and a scone apiece, we relax.

"So, how are the children?" I ask.

"Gemma has met someone in Florida – he seems a nice enough chap, I think she plans to stay out there a bit longer while they decide what they want to do, and Rebecca's little one, Joe, is into everything now. Don't let her know I have told you – she's trying for another baby but so far, no luck. I keep telling her, just be patient and it will happen. I mean, she had Joe without much trouble didn't she? I get worried about her though, she is quite down about it. George's job doesn't help. He is away such a lot these days."

I raise an eyebrow.

"Well, let me know if there is any news and of course I won't mention anything. Not that I ever see her," I laugh because life really has been busy these past couple of years.

"Thank you. I'd love to be a grandma again but if it is just to be to Joe, well, that's fine. I am not sure Rebecca could cope with that though."

"Well, I am sure you'll be sending me good news soon. I haven't anything remotely exciting to tell you I am afraid," I laugh.

She eyes me with what I know to be cousinly concern not pity,

"Don't you ever wish you'd, well…" I know what she is going to say and I cut her off mid flow.

"It just never seemed to be the right time Rachel. You know how I feel about it all…what if, assuming we find this girl, our whole lives are changed? I am sure yours won't, but mine, well, who knows? I know it is silly but I couldn't bear to find that I'd taken something away from them. I don't know if I will remember anything afterwards or if everything will be just the same. Maybe life will go on as though nothing has ever been wrong…but imagine if Ray and I had a child and then, in the blink of an eye, we found we didn't after all? You do understand?"

Rachel sighs and nods, sipping her coffee and wiping the cream from her lips before speaking,

"I know Bea. It's getting close isn't it? To the time when we have to make a decision."

"Very. I keep thinking that we will miss her. After all, what is there to say we will know when she is arriving? We only have a possible year and place to guide us."

"You do know who stays at the cottage though? You have a record?"

"Yes, the cottage is being let out to holiday makers all summer. So far, we haven't had any bookings for the Christmas period. The odd enquiry we have had has come to nothing. To be honest, it has suited us to keep it just for family – it's comforting to know we can pop down there if we feel like it. I know it sounds…morbid but it helps. I handle the bookings these days so I can at least vet every enquiry we do get, the ages and names of any children for instance, that way I hope she won't slip through the net. I've had to make some broad assumptions of course and one of those is to assume the family book it for the Christmas of 2012. That isn't a certainty at all, but we should be able to check if she is with them. We know her Christian name – or at least, we believe we know it, and I have a rough idea of her age."

Rachel is frowning and tapping her coffee cup with the spoon. I wait.

"Are you having second thoughts?"
Her question takes me by surprise, am I? I know Rachel will have noticed the pause,

"No," I say, recovering in an instant , "I won't give up but I have told myself I can't go on forever,"

"How will you judge if it is time to stop though?"

"Well, if the Olympics do go to London in 2012, I will think we are almost there. If nothing happens that

Christmas – I will have to believe that it has all been a vain hope."

"We shall see, then," she nods. I get the feeling that she has no intention of letting this lie, Olympics in London or no.

"It's Athens next," Rachel says.
I am aware of that.

"I suppose, I just have doubts sometimes that anything can be changed I suppose I don't know how I will do it,"
 She interrupts me,

"You'll do it. I know it and so does Nicholas."

"Nicholas? He has never been that keen," I shrug, remembering Nicholas's disparaging comments only last month,

"Looking for your girl from the future again Bea? To be honest, I thought you'd have given up on that one by now. We're all OK aren't we? Let things lie."
Rachel smiles.

"He says he has told you that because if he admits he does have hopes of finding her himself, he will have to admit that all those years he spent getting into trouble and dealing with his guilt, have been a waste of time and he should have done things differently. I think he has believed you since we found the photograph but I think he is also afraid of what might happen when we do find the girl. You should talk to him again. I told him to let you know he is on your side,"

"Oh, I think I know he will support me when it comes to it but I'd just like to think he doesn't think I am a total idiot to pin my hopes on finding this girl. I mean – it does sound impossible, not to mention far-fetched. Who else would believe it?"

"Well, for one thing, the girl," quips Rachel, "Once she has gone back in time,"

I know she is right but I suppose I am frightened by the enormity of what we propose to do.

Rachel pulls out a notebook from her bag and lays it on the table with a flourish. She has built up a profile which she laughs as she calls it, 'Hannah's story," it is all contained within the pages of the notebook she carries with her in her bag. I am less than eager to see it and am sceptical of how accurate it may be. Is it not just a way of passing time, making us feel as though we are doing something when really, there is nothing we can do at the moment? I voice these thoughts and Rachel wags a finger at me,

"It'll be useful, you'll see, when it comes to it. Believe me, Bea, it'll make it easier, to identify her, if it is written down. Just suppose there is another Hannah staying at the cottage – nothing to do with your ghost girl and you put all your energy into getting her to believe she can change things. We might never find this girl!"

I am a little hurt, for the better part of twenty years, I devoted much of my life to looking for clues, to revisiting and re checking events. Isn't it I who have sacrificed so much in search of the moment when time rights itself?

I am reluctant to look at the notebook but I do because Rachel is persuasive and Rachel cares enough to have done this for me. The notes are sparse, the girl is about twelve years old, she has fair hair and a snub nose. She is almost certain to be called Hannah. She wears a sweatshirt emblazoned with the five Olympic rings and the date 2012. She is in the barn at 4 o'clock on Christmas Eve. She is most probably on holiday with her family. She is inquisitive. She is not easily scared. She likes to read. She is thoughtful (she gave someone the card).

"Anything else you can think of that we can add?" she asks. I shrug,

"She was holding something, in her hand, maybe a camera?"

Rachel writes this down and closes the notebook with a flourish.

"I'll take another look at the photograph, see if I can tell exactly what she is holding…"

I am happy for her to carry on collecting what she sees as vital information. It can do no harm and maybe she is right, maybe it will be useful.

My visits home are few and far between. I prefer to meet Dad in town now and again. Our mother is better than she was but still not great. I find it difficult being with her and not telling her about Hannah. Not that she would believe any of it of course. Better she lives in ignorance. This makes me sound heartless I know but after years of trying to help them, I have got to the point of giving up. Besides, part of me believes that their torment will end soon if Rachel and I have got this thing right. Well, at least, I tell myself, it may end. What else but the shooting could have sent them down this fruitless path of self-blame?

Mary's death has changed our lives forever. Yes, hand on heart, I can say I am over the initial grief. I am not over the injustice of it all though and if I still have grief, it is over the waste of Nicholas's younger years as well as the loss of my sister's life.

It will do no good to dwell on things now. Rachel and I need to find out where and when the girl is going to appear.

I must admit, events that have led me full circle to the village I used to live in, have been kind. But then, were they not meant to be? Is this not how it all happened? Perhaps I should not worry about how and why but just concentrate on the way I must help Hannah change things.

Chapter eight

As 1999 moves into Autumn, and the millennium beckons, the world becomes obsessed with what will happen to our computers when the clocks tick over to 2000.

The library has spent a fortune on disaster recovery software and there are fears that our computers will not be able to count from 1999 to 2000. My job is made more difficult by the scaremongering that is going on. Most of the fears will prove to be foundless but we can't take chances. I am so caught up with work that I don't even have time to breathe it seems, let alone worry about where my ghost girl may have come from. 2000 dawns and nothing terrible happens. We all breathe a sigh of relief and for a while, things carry on just as they have done.

It is mid April when Rachel phones me with her good news. Rebecca is pregnant again. The baby is due in early November. I am pleased for her and especially for Rebecca and George. I will become a great aunt again. I am beginning to feel old at the thought.

I am aware that Christmas is growing ever nearer and I make vague plans to include Nicholas in our celebrations this year. He is equally vague about his intentions and I don't press him for an answer. The weeks speed by and we achieve a sense of calm at the library at last. I get home at a reasonable hour each night and my thoughts turn again to Christmas. I really need to make time to get a few presents for my parents although what to get them is not clear. I still harbour a dream of giving them the best Christmas they could ever get. I am trying not to think too much about the ghost girl, as I refer to her for simplicity's sake. To think of her existing now in all probability, makes me shiver in trepidation. I contemplate checking the records for every baby girl born (a parody of Herod perhaps) only in my case, the babies would be girls bearing the name of Hannah. I must not discount all other names of course but I am all but convinced that Hannah will turn out to be her name.

As things turn out, Nicholas is with me when I receive the text from Rachel. He has driven down and intends staying with us for the weekend. It is just as well he has no plans to leave, weather conditions have deteriorated in the last twelve hours. The snow has been falling thick and fast and many of the local roads are closed. We steer clear of talk of ghost girls and of Mary. He tells us he is studying again. Rachel's text comes just as I am getting up to make a pot of tea.

"There has been an accident, George critical, Rebecca went into labour - Baby girl! I am at the hospital. Got to dash. Will keep you informed." she writes. I am shocked. An accident? Poor Rebecca. A frantic call to Gemma, who I know was returning for Christmas with her boyfriend this week, reveals that George was driving back from London when it began to snow heavily. He was taking a different route home due to the snow, lost control of the car and ended up in a ditch. Gemma mentions head injuries and coma. I am horrified. My first instinct is to go to Rachel but she is at the hospital and I am pretty sure the last thing she wants is for me to turn up. She will let me know if anything happens. Meanwhile, I will check on Aunt Jean and make sure she is being kept in the loop. I remember that Christmas from so long ago and a cold chill runs through my veins. Nothing else bad is going to happen to this family is it? That would be just too cruel to contemplate.

As things go, not much happens at all for a long time. Christmas comes and goes. The baby girl does not even get a name for some weeks. Rebecca wants to wait for George to wake up it seems. In the end, she decides to go with the last name they had both liked though had not settled on.

Rachel phones me with the news, her voice, sounding odd with excitement.

"You won't believe it but she's calling the baby Hannah," she whispers.

I am a little taken back but I wouldn't say it calls for much more than mild surprise. How many babies have been called Hannah in the last ten years? How many more will bear that name in the coming months? Rachel refuses to be put off.

"Work it out, Bea. Your girl was about 12 years old in 2012? That's right isn't it?" she didn't wait for me to confirm, "Well, this little girl fits the profile. Remember the one I carry in my bag? I have had this feeling for years Bea, that I am somehow involved, more than just by being a bystander. This does feel like something important."
I agree that perhaps my third cousin could be the child but I can't help thinking, isn't it a bit like looking for the Messiah? Should we really place such expectations on this little scrap of humanity?

"No, not at all. Think how our girl comes to be at the cottage. She must have ties to it somehow. Your parents don't often let it out at Christmas do they?"

It is true, we like to keep Christmas free, just in case one of us wants to be there, to remember. My father used to make it his business to go back every Christmas Eve if he could, just to see, to drive by and maybe put a few ghosts to bed. Maybe he wanted to adjust the clock too. Mother refused. Nick and I have spent a couple of Christmases there, when he was trying to come off the drink. Ray is less keen these days. We have a gorgeous warm and cosy cottage of our own near the pub and the church. We are within spitting distance and can pop back at will if we want to.

"Well, this doesn't mean we should stop looking, it might be her, it could just as well be someone else," I caution.

Rachel has to agree but I can tell she is already sold on the idea that her Hannah will be the girl I saw all those years ago. I go online and do some research when we hang up. It is clear that Hannah has remained a popular name for several years although, if anything, it has dwindled in popularity this year, in favour of such diverse and grandiose names as Olivia and Madison.

Rachel's treasured profile stands up pretty well, I have to admit. She has built it up from the notes made when I first described Hannah to her, all those years ago but she has amended it over time, as certain things have become clear over the years. There was the advent of the photograph for one thing followed by mobile phones and computers for instance. Things we had neither understood nor thought important, became obvious. Hannah's clothing, the sweatshirt she was wearing with the date and the Olympic rings, the object becoming visible in her hand as she stands there, cocooned in shadow. It all puts her in the correct time frame.

Now, of course, Rachel is bound to put two and two together and make five. How do I know she didn't influence her daughter's choice of name? But would that matter? I am having difficulty seeing what is meant to be and what we are changing. It is hard to focus on the necessary without becoming embroiled with the what-ifs and the maybes. I know Rachel would not knowingly have influenced their choice of name of course. I consider the possibility for a while. It would not be so amazing would it? We are talking about a girl who was at Angel Cottage at a time when to date, only family have stayed. It does not require such a giant leap of the imagination to place my third cousin at the scene does it?

I visit Rebecca and Hannah while they are staying with Rachel. George is still in hospital of course but making slow progress. The baby is sweet. She is fairish but it is hard to connect her with the child she will become. Rachel is jumping up and down with excitement at the prospect before her—to think that her granddaughter could hold the key. I know she will be keeping close tabs on the girl and feel a little guilty. All I can do is wait, just as I have been doing for the past thirty years or so.

"She thinks what?" Nicholas is gob smacked, "She thinks her granddaughter is the flippin' Messiah?"

"Nicholas, please!" I am smiling but I don't want him to dismiss the notion because she could be the one, she could, I am certain. By now I have begun to think like Rachel. The girl must have some common ties with the cottage or she would not be there. Our parents have never been keen on letting the place out at Christmas.

"It's for family," they say when I have questioned them, just to check, just to be sure.

Nicholas and I have met up, quite unusual for us, to discuss our parents' deteriorating relationship. We both think they should make an effort and either pull together once and for all or break up for good. Their constant bickering and separation, during which time they expect to stay with one of us, is wearing us down. I will be fifty soon enough. Enough is enough. It's time to face facts. They just don't seem to be any good for one another anymore. Both are well into their seventies, can they not agree to differ and rub along together like other married couples or call it a day? I do wonder if things might have been different without the accident but really, even allowing for that, they are a pretty toxic mix.

"Well, I suppose the whole thing is so preposterous, one more ridiculous idea won't hurt," he says. I do wish he would admit that he feels just the same about this as us. I ignore the jibe and continue relating Rachel's latest revelation.

"So, this baby, does she look anything like your girl from the future, yeah, I know, our girl from the future," he holds up his hands in mock surrender.

I laugh, "Not at the moment, she looks like any other baby. The right colouring I suppose and the right name…but if she isn't the one, I have to believe that the real Hannah will put in an appearance at the right time."

"So, it's a case of, will the real Hannah please stand up?"

"Something like that. What we have to remember is, it has happened hasn't it? It won't unhappen by itself."

"I think you will find that is not even a word Madam Literature expert," he raises an eyebrow.

I allow him to smile. One day he will see that we have been right to wait, right to hope and right to believe.

"Any more thoughts on what might happen to us though, Bea? If everything changes? We could be playing with fire," he is at once serious.

I know my face drops as he reminds me of this dangerous conundrum. We only know this way of life. If one thing changes, what will happen to everything else? Will we set up a ripple effect that spreads beyond our family? I have struggled with this concept over the years as much as him but I always come to the same conclusion.

"It isn't down to us, not really. Think of what has already happened to us, to Mary, because one thing was changed years ago, that shouldn't have been changed. Hannah should never have gone back in time. She is the one who should not change things." I pause, "If we stopped her from going back now, she wouldn't be changing anything."

"Right, so Hannah has already been back, changed things before she was born…but what if that was meant to be? What if this is how it is meant to be for us?" he sits back and shakes his head, "Phew! I just hope we aren't opening up a can of worms…suppose she went back and changed something else before, something we aren't aware of that stops a world war or prevents a deadly epidemic? We stop her now and all hell breaks loose."

"Ok, so we don't stop her, we let her go to the cottage and do whatever it is she does but this time, we make sure Buster doesn't get into the barn. It was Buster jumping at you that made the gun fire remember. That was just after I saw her, in the corner of the barn. I wish you remembered more. I wish you had seen her too."

We pass a pleasant enough evening, talking about this ridiculous yet not so ridiculous plan we have hatched based on something that I know happened and he doesn't remember,

"As it happens, I do remember," he admits when we are opening another bottle of wine.
I stare at him open mouthed.

"You saw her too?"

"I think so. Not in the barn, except later in the photo of course. I saw her in the cottage. I thought it was you or Mary at first but you were both in the kitchen and this girl sort of appeared and disappeared by the fireplace."

"Why didn't you say anything?"

"Because I thought I'd imagined it. Later, I thought you had been playing tricks and then I suppose I just forgot. I didn't even think of it when you said you'd seen someone in the barn. By the time I realised I might have seen the same girl, it was all over and we were moving and I didn't want to admit I'd seen anything in case you all laughed at me and thought I was trying to pass the blame."

"You were not to blame," I say facing him with a level stare.

"Well, you'd feel to blame if you had been the one who had held the gun,"
I couldn't argue with that.

"So, the photo convinced you?" I ask softly.

"It did but it scared me too. Consequences Bea, there are always consequences. I worry about these things. It's hard to be me sometimes you know."

I let him go on a bit before we agree to talk about something else. It is draining to keep going over and over the one subject.

The phone rings at a quarter to ten that evening. It is Rachel.

"George is coming home," she says.

Chapter nine

Ray and I have been living back in my childhood village for a whole year by the time George goes home. The time has gone almost too fast. We have been accepted back into the community as though we have never left. The initial whispers and furtive looks soon disappear. People accept that we are more than that infamous family whose brother shot his sister. There are not too many people left who remember the tragic accident and those that do say little about it. It is not long before the more curious also leave us alone and village gossip turns to other things.

I am glad to be back where I can see what is going on with Angel Cottage. It has been well occupied throughout the summer but we get to pop back there and keep an eye on things in between bookings. Now that winter is approaching once again, there are jobs to be done, paintwork to be refreshed, carpets to be cleaned. It is good to see that so much remains the same.

One late Autumn afternoon, when the last guests have long since left, I drive down the road to Angel Cottage. I stroll across the courtyard and let myself in the kitchen. There is a chill in the air. I pull my cardigan closer and push the door to. The Angel clock still sits on the wall opposite the cooker. It is still running fast. I step up to it and gingerly push the hands back.

"Come on Mary, we are waiting," I whisper as I do so. There is no one to hear me. The clock ticks on.

I look around me. I would put an AGA here if this was my kitchen, I muse. I run my hand across the work tops. The surfaces have been cleaned and gleam beneath the lights.

There are a few concessions to the present day but not many. There is no internet connection for example nor is there a landline. There is a freezer, something we did not have as children and the kitchen table has been varnished but the marks from dozens of pairs of hands still adorn it beneath the glaze. I cross to the sink and gaze out of the window. A bird sings in the tree beyond the window, I wonder what he sees. Does he fly in this time or does he dip in and out of another? Not for the first time, I wonder what it is that carries Hannah through the time window. Is it the clock? Is it some sort of dimensional collision?

I have been studying details of full moons, eclipses, storms and even earthquakes, checking where they occur and what impact they might have on this small part of the world. It fascinates me. To date, I have not come up with anything startling. The only physical phenomenon connecting everything, as far as I can see, is snow. It snowed that fateful Christmas and it snowed when George had his accident. I am pretty sure Hannah had snowflakes in her hair but from our time or hers? I struggle with the finer points of this but then I don't know why I even bother. I know that what happens will just happen…won't it?

If I can change just one small part of it though. That's the bit that escapes me really. If I find the girl, can I warn her? Won't she think me mad? If the girl is Rebecca's Hannah does that make it easier or more difficult? I frequently hurt my head trying to second guess everything.

I have not come here just to go over events again though. My purpose today is to go into the attic and see exactly what is up there. I promised my father I would make a proper inventory. Besides, I remember there being a couple of lamps which I would quite like to take back for our cottage. I find the lamps but as I move them, I see the box of decorations pushed to the far side of the attic. I take a deep breath and slide it towards me. I haven't looked inside it since that fateful Christmas. I open the box and slip my hand in. I pull out a length of tinsel. I feel no emotion and delve deeper. What am I looking for? I laugh at myself, there is nothing here of real interest. I promised Ray I would not be too long. I close the box and push it back against the wall. As I walk down the steps, the lamps safe in my arms, I belatedly remember the Angel. The Christmas Angel was not in the box of course. So, where is it? Perhaps I can find it. We never did give the barn a proper search, did we? It would be nice to have the angel back in her place at the top of a tree. I leave the lamps on the back seat of the car and head to the barn.

I have been here several times in recent years. My initial reluctance finally gave way to curiosity. Still, always, I have to steel myself to open that door and put my foot inside. Always, I am struck by the sense of unease that fills this place. If I had to describe it to someone, I might say it was unsettled, waiting. Of course, that could just be my imagination but I might be forgiven for attributing such feelings to an inanimate place, considering what has occurred here.

Now, I close the heavy door behind me and flick the switch so that darkness swirls into light.
The ladder is still there. I climb it, rueful at the effort it takes. At almost fifty, I do not have quite the agility of my younger self. Still, I haul myself up onto the hayloft floor, stooping a little to avoid the low beams and there, right in front of me, is the trunk of old clothes. A few feet to its left, sits the rocking horse, blind in one eye, and there is the old fort. It all looks very reassuring and familiar. A childhood encapsulated.

I try not to look at the floorboards where Mary fell. Whoever had the task of removing the blood, did a good job but there is still the faintest darkening of the boards where she fell. I turn away.

I touch the lid of the trunk. I have a key for it now. The barn has been out of bounds for guests but still, some things need to be locked. I turn the key and lift the lid. Someone has taken care to fold and wrap the garments in tissue paper. Did mother do this? I can't imagine it but perhaps, when she was mourning Mary in those first months, she found some solace in handling the clothes her daughter had last been handling. They give me no solace whatsoever. I have no interest in them but I have to see if the Angel is beneath them. It was forgotten about in the terrible aftermath but it has niggled me since. Was it there? If we had not played around with the clothes but had carried on looking, would we have found it and been out of the barn before anything could happen?

After a few minutes, I have pulled out every last garment. I stare at the bottom of the trunk. A crumpled package sits there. The Christmas Angel. I pick it up and replace the clothes, sitting back on my heels. I try to imagine what Hannah will see when she walks into the barn. Will she see what I am seeing at first? Or will she see a group of children playing, straight away? I don't know how this will work. I think about leaving a message on the door to the barn, a clue, a warning. I can't think what. I feel the slight weight of the Christmas Angel in my hand and toy with the idea of returning it to the box of decorations. Isn't that why I was looking for it? I hesitate. It wouldn't be right to take it I feel. I open the trunk and lay it back within the folds of material. Let it stay there. I cannot explain why I had to find it, nor why, now that I have, I am leaving it here. It is just something I am drawn to do.

As I tread down the ladder, I feel a shiver run down my spine. A memory awakened perhaps? A sense of closure maybe? In a very short time, I will have closure in one form or another. I cannot believe that the time has come.

I am about to switch the light off and make my way back to the cottage when I remember the diary. Will it still be where I left it? I remember writing in it with such fury in those first few weeks after Mary's death. I was twelve years old, it was pretty humdrum on the whole, as diaries go, until that final entry.

It seems so long ago now that I wrote those final pages, numb with grief. I remember the urgency with which I committed word to paper. The diary was the only eye witness account there was. The newspaper reports, they just guessed at what had happened, the police pieced together a picture from the things we said but that diary was the real evidence and I hid it. Of course, I know its exact location. I remember what I did with it. I hope it will still be there. No one knew I had hidden it and I don't suppose anyone realises that I ever wrote it. The very nature of a diary is secrecy, after all.

As the years rolled by, I all but forgot about it to be honest. Now, standing here, I decide to go and find it. With a backward glance at the ladder, I cross the dusty floor and push the barn door open. Emerging into the muted sunshine of Autumn, I blink and head back to the cottage.

My old room is much the same as it always was, the same wardrobe, the same chest of drawers beneath the window. Only the bed is new, bought when we began letting the place out. The new house had had fitted cupboards and drawers. I pull open the bottom drawer and reach behind it. I am half afraid that the thing will have gone. Who would remove a drawer and search behind it? I pull the drawer free and roll back the carpet beneath. The floorboard, loosened when the place was rewired while Grandma Lu still lived here, lifts without a problem. I slide it to one side and delve deep beneath the layers of insulation, pulling out the small notebook that was my diary. No one has found it then. Part of me is a little disappointed. Have I wanted it to be found? I realise that I have harboured that hope. If someone had found it, maybe they would have taken up the quest to free Mary. That's how I view her death now, something that was not real, something that has just kept her from us.

My hands push the board back into place, press the carpet down and refit the drawer in one swift movement. Taking a deep breath, I open the book and sit back on my heels.

The childish writing is neat and well formed. I am twelve years old again. Outside a dog barks. Is that Buster? I wonder if he comes and goes through time too, then chide myself for being ridiculous. I have it, the diary I wrote in, full of faith, all those years ago. I spend a minute or two just running my fingers over the grainy cover. I lift it to my nose and sniff the pages. Never have been able to resist the smell of paper. This, I remember, used to smell of fresh cotton. Now, it smells a little musty. I wrinkle my nose in mild distaste. Well, it has lain here untouched for some considerable time, after all.

I have forgotten the codicil I put at the beginning, the day I hid it. It leaps out at me now as I turn the first page.

"They think I am mad, they think I believe in ghosts,"

I smile. Preposterous, they said, ridiculous, a load of rubbish but I believed and I still believe, that the day will come when my ghost girl will appear again and this time, I will be ready for her.

After a while, I make the decision to take the book with me. An idea has taken root in my mind. It will take time to ferment. Still, I am glad I have the diary. I think I know what I will do with it. I take a last look at the barn as I lock the cottage door. Now shadowed by the setting sun, it looks as though it belongs to another world, another time. I laugh at myself and make my way back to my car. Once in the driver's seat, I take a deep breath and pat my pocket to check I have not dropped the diary. It is still there, safe and bursting with the promise of the answer to this puzzle, I am sure. The inventory is forgotten for now.

I spray the windscreen, clearing it of its cache of autumn insects and watch as the water runs down the screen, like tears. For a reason unknown to me, I am at once transported to that stair well when I was twelve years old, listening to the rain and discovering Schrödinger's Cat. How much sense it made to me then. Quantum Theory is something I later studied in more depth. Always, I came to the same conclusion. For as long as the barn remains locked in that time and place, until Hannah releases it by stepping back through time, then nothing has happened. Mary is both dead and alive.

Mary's fate remains unknown. Nicholas used to argue against me for hours. He has given up now and I like to think that some of my certainty has made it into his head. The closer we get to that fateful day, the more stable his character seems to become. Is that a good sign? What will happen to him if we are wrong and come Christmas Eve 2012, Mary is still dead?

I give a brief thought to Hannah who may have to witness that dreadful tragedy. It is not something I am happy about but then again, she has already witnessed it has she not? In my world at least. I have no control over that, if it must happen. I can only hope that it does not happen. The riddle seems to grow ever more complicated, the nearer the time for its conclusion gets. I spray the windscreen one last time and reverse the car out of the drive.

George gets a new job and he and Rebecca move house. Rachel tells me it is because they have been having some problems. He is still not himself and they are finding life tough. They think that by moving somewhere different, they will have a fresh start.

"Perhaps it isn't meant to be," she murmurs. This is the first time I have ever heard her doubt this thing that we have both so heavily invested in. It is ironic that I am more positive now. The link is too strong to be broken by a simple move. Rachel still lives a stone's throw from me and I am as close to the cottage as I can be without setting up camp in the field behind.

"It's meant to be," I tell her and she nods, raising her little finger and linking mine just as we did all those years ago…

"Soulmates," she whispers.

Will she and I be so close if this thing works? Will our relationship change? I don't know. I hope there is more to hold us together than the events of Christmas 1963.

Chapter ten
July 2005

It is a warm July day, when we tune into the radio to hear the official announcement. Everyone in the library is eager to hear where the next Olympic games will be held. I say nothing, I have more reason than most to hope to hear the words I need to hear. We all know just how much the British team have put into this bid. IOC president, Jacques Rogge, makes the dramatic announcement at 12.49 pm.

A great cheer goes up across the library as the news is broadcast. There is almost a party atmosphere in the building. Prime Minister Tony Blair, calls the win, "a momentous day" for Britain. I listen to the words and something inside me twists. This is indeed a momentous occasion. This proves to me that there is still hope.

Rachel and I swap texts. The ease with which we communicate these days means that we no longer have the need for lengthy conversations. A simple,

"Have you heard?"

"Yes, London 2012!"

"Things are going to happen,"

suffices.

There are now seven years to get through, seven years in which any of us could make a mistake that puts an end to this agonising wait once and for all. Now that it is all beginning to seem so real, I am feeling nervous. This is no longer wishful thinking, the girl in the photograph, Hannah, is real, the date on the sweater, real, I have to lie down and close my eyes when I get home, just to come to terms with all of this.

I have to tell myself that it could still all come to nothing though. Perhaps nothing will happen. Perhaps Hannah will not get to the barn in time. This thought is quashed as fast as it is born. Of course she will make it. It has already happened.

I consider again, the merits of preventing her being there. Would that simply put us all back where we were before the accident? Would Mary have lived? I go over and over it in my mine but I always come to the same conclusion. Hannah must go into the barn and make certain.

Now I just need to sit back and wait for something to happen. Seven years is a long time but I will need time to prepare.

By coincidence, I am transferred to the main branch in Southampton for a three-month period running up to Christmas, holiday cover they call it. This takes me within a couple of miles of Rebecca and George and I mean to call in and say hello. I even get as far as picking up the phone to call but something stops me. Perhaps it is Rachel's assertion that Becky is finding things hard at the moment and a slight feeling of guilt that Rachel and I are pinning our hopes on Hannah being the one. I am not sure what support I can offer right now.

The one time I do pluck up the courage to knock on the door, no one is home and after that, work becomes manic and I am not in the mood for visiting afterwards, I just want to get home to Ray and snuggle up by the fire.
A week before Christmas, I volunteer to go and buy some holly and mistletoe for the staff room. The stuff they are selling near the library is tired and old. It will give me a chance to have a breather.

"Try the Garden Centre, they have loads!" someone suggests.

Half an hour later, I am parked outside the Garden Centre, wondering whether or not to get out of the car just yet as it has begun to snow a little and I have left my coat behind. My old red jumper is on the back seat. I pull it on over my work clothes and find my gloves.

I can see the Christmas trees laid out for inspection. I'd buy one but there is no way I can get one of those in my little car. Besides, we have had an artificial tree for the past few years. I take a look anyway, just to smell them. I am disappointed that they don't smell particularly,

"Been treated love," a man tells me with a knowing nod.

I am walking towards the section where the holly is on display, when the car drives in. The headlights blind me for a second and I turn away but when I turn back I see that it is George who is driving. Rachel has told me he is back at work and driving again. He looks far better than the last time we crossed paths.

I don't think he will know who I am, we didn't speak much at Rachel's that time, but I am on the verge of introducing myself when my attention is caught by someone with him. A small, fair haired girl steps out of the car and is examining the prone trees with an eagerness afforded the very young. I am transfixed.

I know I am staring but I can't help myself. The child not fifty feet from me, is the spitting image of my ghost girl. Yes, a few years younger but…it is her, I am sure. George appears to be losing patience. The girl is trying her best. I bite my lip and step forward. I must get a closer look.

"What about this one?" I ask, holding up a tree that looks ok to me,

She smiles straight at me and I find myself beaming back so that she is a little disconcerted. Oh dear, I didn't mean to frighten the child yet she is no ghost, she is here and very much alive. At that moment, her life seems a tenuous thing and I am worried for her safety within this outrageous plan of ours. Checking myself, I try to remain calm.

George is thanking me and I think that perhaps he does recognize me for a moment but he is trying to pay me, he thinks I work here. I put him right of course and there is my cue to say who I am. I don't.

"Thank you," she beams and trots after her father who pays the man at the desk. I cannot leave, not until they have driven out of sight, the tree slung on the roof rack. She must think me mad, staring after them like that. I shake myself out of my trance-like state and start the engine. I forget all about the holly and mistletoe so that I arrive back at the library empty handed and have to nip out to the market and pick up some straggly bits and bobs that will do the trick.

As soon as I have a free moment, I text Rachel.

"I have seen her. It's her, I am sure of it."

"Really? I knew it! Did you speak?"

"No, not really…"

We swap texts for of course we are excited. No photo she has ever sent me convinced me as much as this meeting. In the photographs, I really thought the resemblance to Mary was what I was seeing. Now I know. I was seeing the ghost girl all along.

I have questions to ask, plenty of them when Rachel and I meet up a week later, for a Christmas meal.

"Should I spend time with her do you think?"

"I don't see that that would do any good. It might be stressful for you and for her. I talk about you and Becky knows the story of what happened…"

"And?" I don't want to hear what is coming,

"In her words, she thinks you are a little bats. Oh, don't worry," she adds with a hasty smile," she thinks I am a little batty too, for believing you,"

"She knows what we think happened back then?"

"Well, she knows that you say you saw a ghost and that I believe you. She doesn't know that we think Hannah has anything to do with it. I am sure it is her and you are sure it is her but could you really expect anyone else to believe us?"

I shake my head.

"No, well, I feel if you did spend a lot of time with Hannah, you might scare her off before she can do anything. This has to be something that happens naturally, from her point of view. If we push her too much, she may close up. She can be very stubborn you know, but she is sensible too. I think we just let her be for a while."
I do. I have been thinking the same. I don't think I could cope with seeing Hannah beyond the odd family visit. Best not to get too close as Rachel says.

There is not much danger of that as it happens. With them living such a distance away and me working, opportunities are thin on the ground.

My time at the library in Southampton comes to an end and I am back at my local branch for Christmas itself. Becky and George and Hannah and Joe are staying with Rachel for a couple of days. Ray and I are invited but in a rare moment of togetherness, my parents have already asked us to join them for Christmas dinner. It seems cruel not to go if they are making such an effort. We make plans to go to Rachel's on Boxing Day.

My parents are remarkably normal, that's the first thing I notice about them, as we enter the house. They both look smart and my mother has had her normally lank hair styled by the looks of things. She is wearing lipstick and for a moment, I see the Marjorie I remember from childhood. I am struck by how thin she is but no one can deny she is making an effort here. My father, forever the gentleman, takes our coats and makes us a drink. My mother chooses water. This act alone is enough to alert me to the change in her.

I corner my father in the kitchen as he is decanting the wine,

"So, what's happening with Mum?" I ask.

"She's trying, she's not had a drink for at least six months. She has cut out her tablets and she is really trying…" he looks nervous I realise. They are on trial here. This is the first time we have been over for dinner in, years. Other visits have not been the best and now, here they are, if appearances are anything to go by, having turned a corner. I smile and touch his arm,

"It's great Dad, really. You both look, good," I reach up and peck him on the cheek.

"Thanks pumpkin," he grins and for a moment I am five years old again, standing in the kitchen, watching him make me a cocoa while mother puts Nicholas to bed. I am happier than I remember being for a long time seeing them doing so well after all these years. Both are now in their seventies. I am proud of them. I give him a hug and we go back into the dining room where Ray is having a proper conversation with my mother about the garden. It is almost surreal.

Afterwards, Ray and I discuss the change that has come over my parents and decide that time really does cure most things.

"It's a shame it won't bring Tom back," he sighs.
I nod, "At least he and Rachel were happy, all the time," I tell him.

We make it over to Rachel's on Boxing Day. She is there with Gemma and we get to meet the new man in Gemma's life at long last, Toby.

"Heard a lot about you," Toby says in a perfect English accent. I am a little surprised, I had thought, Gemma having met him in Florida, he would be American,

"Nope, British through and through, born in Islington. I was over there on a research grant, same as Gem," he tells me.

Gemma flashes her ring finger at me and I smile in delight, a diamond catches the light and she giggles in a way belying her thirty two years. There will be a wedding soon then, I surmise.

"So, how were your parents?" Rachel is eager to hear about the previous day. I tell her and she is as amazed as we were at the change that has been wrought over Marjorie and Charles. Toby raises an eyebrow when he hears. Has he been told the full story? I am pretty sure he will have had the gist of it told him.

"How is George doing?" I enquire when the moment is right.

"Oh, you know, he struggles on. I think he finds the new job a bit much but he is coping well, all things considered. Becky is doing her best too…" her voice trails off and I detect worry there.

"What's wrong with Becky?" I ask when we are alone, washing up in the kitchen,

"Well, she's worn out I think. The accident, the children, looking after George all these years and well, he isn't the easiest to live with you know. She has this tablet to help her sleep, that tablet to help her get through the day…I worry about them and now they are so far away, I can't keep an eye on them."

"Poor Becky," I murmur, "Life's a bitch eh?"
Rachel smiles and touches my arm,

"You are not wrong!" she observes and we fall silent for a while, each contemplating how our lives have turned out.

"That's right, isn't it Mum?" Gemma is calling as we go back in the sitting room,

"What's that?" Rachel asks.

"Hannah, she calls her parents Becky and George. That's right isn't it?"

"Oh, yes, she always has done, not to their faces but when she is talking about them. I am so used to it I don't even think about it I must say but it is a little strange. Her therapist…"

"She has a therapist?" I am shocked,

"Well, she has these nightmares…they reckon they have been brought on by the accident but I blame them on her and Becky not bonding as they should have when she was tiny...don't look at me like that Gemma, you know it is true. Those children suffered a lot when George was ill and I am not blaming Becky, she did what she thought best,"

"It must have been very difficult," I say, "But they had you, that must have helped Rachel,"

"Yes, they had me," she sighs, "It might be good that they have to do without me for a while, I think they were becoming dependent on me, as was Becky, though I hate to say it."

"Whew, sounds tough," Toby observes and we all nod.

"And what does she call you, Rachel?" I ask.

"Oh, she calls me Gran, always has. When I think of the night she was born, Becky was torn between her new born daughter and the husband she thought was dying. It was a dreadful time you know. I sat and held that baby then and it seems I have been doing that ever since."

Her sigh reveals much about the past few years, years I have not really known all that much about. I feel a little selfish that I have spent all my energy on this quest for putting right something that happened so long ago, when all

154

the time, Rachel has been going through all sorts right under my nose.

"George is on the mend though," Gemma says with a rueful grin, "He'll always have a limp and his mood swings might not get much better but everything else," she taps her head, "is working,"

The conversation is steered away from George after that. I think Rachel realises that we are treading dangerous ground here.

When Rachel and I are next alone, washing up the coffee cups in her immaculate kitchen, I bring up the subject once again.

"How is all this affecting Hannah?" I ask.

"Oh, she's a bright little thing, knows how things are and in a funny kind of way, I think it has helped her develop into a very caring and helpful little girl. One good thing that has come out of it. We are very close."
I am not sure how to take that last remark. Is she warning me not to mess with Hannah?

"I am sure she is, don't worry, I won't seek her out on purpose or anything. But, I have found my diary…the one I wrote when it all happened. I thought that maybe she should read it someday, someday before…"
Rachel is nodding and lays a hand on my arm,

"That would be a very good idea, she loves reading but she is still only five years old, wait a few years maybe?"
I smile and nod. I have already formed a plan in my own head and know exactly when I will give Hannah that diary.

It will be cutting it fine and it will rely on her reading it bcfore she goes into the barn but I will do it. In the meantime, I will stay away. There is no need for our paths to cross more than is necessary in the next few years.

All the way home, Ray shakes his head.

"What?" I ask.

"You," he says,

"Me?"

"Yes, you. You don't think I don't know what you and Rachel are cooking up between you? Come on Bea, this obsession you both have and now you think Hannah has something to do with it?"

I don't say anything. How does he know these things? How has he heard? Of course, he could have overheard us in the kitchen just now but it is probable he has heard any number of conversations over the years and put two and two together.

"We shall see," is all I manage.

I would like Ray to be on side, I want him to know everything but there is little point. In a few years, the truth will come out one way or another. It occurs to me at that very moment that perhaps we won't remember the truth or we won't remember what went before. What then? Well, I console myself, if that is the way it has to be then so be it. We will at least be happy. Somewhere in my mind, I think about Hannah and what this may do to her if anything. She is family after all. She is connected to all this.

When I have some time to spare, I spend a while going over the major events of the past few years and trying to determine what would be different.

Ray and I met while I was at University. He had nothing to do with the accident, nor did my meeting him depend on it. I am sure I would have chosen this route in any case. In fact, my days at University were perhaps, the only days in which I did not spend most of my waking moments thinking about Mary. I was living in a bubble. I don't think things would have turned out any different had Mary lived.

I cannot be sure but I think Ray and I would have met, fallen in love and married in any case. Would there have been children? I did not make the conscious choice not to have a family. It just never happened. Neither of us felt the need and neither felt it to be the fault of the other. It is just one of those things. Maybe it is something that was never meant to be. I, of all people, should be able to cope with that.

When it does happen, it is funny how unprepared I really am. It is Christmas again.
This year, I am putting up decorations in the cottage because I have done so every year since I found out for sure who Hannah is. As far as I know, Rachel is staying with Becky and George. I asked Rachel to join us but she had already promised to be with her grandchildren.
It is with trepidation that I dress the tree.

Will this be the year? I cannot see how, considering Hannah will be in Hampshire but suppose we have been wrong all along and it is another girl who will come looking? I have to be ready.

Nicholas is staying with us. He has spent the last three Christmases with us in fact. I really believe he has stopped drinking so much (I think our parents were the trigger for that). He has been sober for four years now or as he likes to put it,

"I have been of this world for four years," The rest of the time, he tells me, he has been out of it.

I am battling with our own Christmas tree, trying to get it to stand up straight, when the phone rings. It is Rachel. She sounds a little breathless.

"Bea? It's me, there's been a change of plan. How is the cottage fixed for visitors?"
I wonder if there has been a family argument, is Rachel now on her own? Of course, she must stay with us if that's the case.

"No, Bea, all of us, not just me. Becky thinks it'll do us all good to have a break and she thought of the cottage. I said I'd enquire if it was free, it is I take it?"

For a moment, I don't speak.

"Bea, you still there?"

"Yes, of course, So that includes, Joe and Hannah too?" I am incredulous. Is this how simple it will be?

"Well, Joe is not too keen but he'll come around and yes, Hannah too, of course Hannah too. She is really looking forward to it. She's never been there you see, has she?"

I am almost rendered speechless.

They are coming. Hannah is coming. I put the phone down and feel my heart thudding against my chest. Where is Nick?

"What on earth's the matter? Having trouble with the lights?" he quips as he comes into the room. I realise I am still clutching the phone. I lay it in its holder and turn to face him. I take a deep breath.

"Hannah will be at the cottage on Christmas Eve," I blurt out.

"Whoa! Who arranged that?"

"Well, Becky as it happens, she asked Rachel to ask me. What do you think?"

"I think, this could either be the biggest let down since Take That broke up or it could be the best thing since sliced bread," he grins.

"This calls for a bit of a celebration, something special," I tease.

He regards me with a quizzical look.

With a flourish, I reach into the bureau drawer and retrieve the diary. Waving it in front of his face, I give a broad grin.

"It's time to get this out and start things off," I say, my voice wavering a little as the enormity of what I am saying, hits me. Nicholas blows his breath out through his teeth but says nothing. Ray on the other hand looks worried.

In the privacy of our bedroom he studies me as I undress.

"You could be setting yourself up for a fall, you know," he says at length.

"I know, don't worry. I am going into this with my eyes wide open," I assure him, whilst inside, I am not so sure at all.

"Ok, but if nothing happens, if this crazy idea proves to be just that, a crazy idea, promise me, you will be content and happy with just me?"
I survey him with surprise, my eyes welling up,

"Of course I will, darling, I have been content and happy all these years."

"Yes, but you have been so caught up with this, this crusade, this forty or fifty-year pilgrimage…sometimes I have felt that if it all comes to nothing, there won't be anything left for me."

I consider this for a moment. It is not as ridiculous as it sounds. I always tell myself I am leading life to the full but am I? So much time has been taken up with this quest, this impossible yet altogether possible, search. I am mortified that I may have led Ray to feel this way. I cross the room and take him in my arms. We cling together as though we are expecting to be torn apart at any moment. I feel the warmth of his body against mine, the certainty of his being, the safety of being wrapped in his arms.

"Do you ever stop to think what it will be like if we do change things?" I ask him, after a while. We have never discussed this subject before, not at any length. I didn't realise he knew so much about it. He buries his nose in my hair,

"I don't pretend to understand and I don't pretend to believe this is possible but if we assume that you and Rachel are right and by Christmas eve afternoon I will have a sister-in-law, you will have your sister and everything we know now may change…how do we know that you and I will even be together still? Will we have ever met?"

I squeeze him tight. I share his fear but I don't tell him. Part of me wants to abandon ship right now. Despite the years of waiting and wondering that have gone before, I remember the years of struggle, the awful years with Nicholas going off the rails and our parents' gradual decline as they drifted apart. I remember the terrible sense of disbelief as Mary fell. The awful ordeal of the hospital and the police questions, the grief. What can be worse than that?

"What will you do?" he asks, as though I have a plan. I am shocked to realise that I have no plan beyond giving Hannah my diary and hoping she will see through it. I comfort myself with the thought that she did see me the day before that fatal accident, she will remember that, she will know I am warning her. She won't think me mad.

Why don't I just go and explain it all to her? Why do I not take her to one side and say, look Hannah, you are about to have an amazing experience. You are going to walk into 1963 and see me as a young girl. The thing is, you are also going to cause the death of my sister unless you stop the dog from getting into the barn. I could do that but Rachel and I have discussed this and both of us feel it would be unfair to put this burden on Hannah. What if it goes wrong? We may have scarred her for life.

There is little we can do to prevent her from being there, that much we have agreed, short of locking her in her room for Christmas. Why did we not just prevent her from going to the cottage and save ourselves and further grief? That too has been discussed but we agreed, we will just let things take their natural course. All I will do is warn Hannah, somehow . My head spins with the thoughts that tumble around in it but I have a plan.

"Hey, just relax will you?" pleads Ray and I do, just for a little while. Tomorrow is another day, tomorrow is Christmas Eve.

Christmas Eve dawns cold and crisp. A smattering of snow has already fallen and the ground is hard beneath my feet. I am crossing the courtyard. The kitchen door is opened, Rachel has seen me walking up the path.

"Come in, come in," she says, her face every bit as anxious as my own and I am at once drawn into the bosom of her family. George is stirring soup on the stove, Becky is sitting at the table, wrapping a present, Joe is curled up on the settle in the corner with his phone playing some game or other but Hannah is nowhere to be seen.

"Sorry to call at this hour," I say.

"Oh no, that's fine, really, Happy Christmas!" says Becky. Rachel smiles at me and pulls out a chair,

"Do sit down," she says, with a formal air that makes me smile, adding, "I'll go get Hannah, she will love to meet you." If her daughter gives her a strange look, it passes without comment.

Rachel and Joe, slip out of the house and hurry across to the barn. A slight panic grips me. Am I too late? I check the clock. No, there is plenty of time, there has to be. A moment later and Rachel propels Hannah into the room.

"This is Hannah," Becky says, "Hannah, this is Mrs Carmichael, your Gran's cousin," Hannah wriggles from her grasp. She smiles at me and mutters a meek, "Hello," For a moment I think she recognizes me but the moment passes.

I pull the book out of my pocket and put it on the table, pushing it towards the child.

"I thought you might like to read this," I say.

Hannah takes the diary and looks at it with a puzzled frown.

"It was written by a girl who used to live in this cottage," I push, "she was about your age and I think she would like you to read it."

She mentions the Diary of Anne Frank, they have been reading that at school. I cannot pretend my diary compares to that but it does beg to be read.

"Are you sure she won't mind? It's a diary," she says with a dubious look at the cover.

"I know she would love you to read it," I say. I can see the curiosity light up her eyes. I bite my lip, I won't say anything more.

"Thank you," and she clutches the book close. I imagine she will disappear into the snug when I have gone and will curl up on the leather sofa and read. I feel I know her far better than I do. She was holding a book when I saw her in the snug that time. The memory has sprung unasked into my mind. Is it a sign that things are beginning to change? Is she seeing me now? I cannot cope with the knowledge. I must get out of here and hope that Rachel will do her part. We have agreed, no forcing the issue. What will be will be. I just hope that this time it will be different.

Chapter eleven

Hannah 2012

I put Beatrice's diary down and stare at it, the last page still open on my lap. The last line, like the first, reads,

"They think I am mad, they think I believe in ghosts,"

I don't think she is mad. There is something that rings true about what she has written. I wish I had the internet here and then I might Google it. As it is, all I can do is ask around. Becky and George won't know anything and there's Joe of course but Mrs Carmichael must know something and she has given me the diary for a reason, that much is obvious. Does she think I know something about all this? I feel a little dizzy having read the entire thing. It is all there, Beatrice's story. From the outset, it is clear it is set in Angel cottage. It is also obvious that her vivid imagination has played a big part in what she has written between these pages. For goodness sake, who would believe anyone could travel through time and change history?

I place the diary on the coffee table and stare at it for a while. I am sitting on the very same sofa that Beatrice sat on when she saw this strange apparition. Could it be the same girl I have seen? Have we both seen this ghost? I chew this over for a bit in my mind before the penny drops. Beatrice was writing about me.

The realisation hits me like a bolt from the blue. I am stunned, this is me? I am the one who opens the barn door? I am the girl Beatrice saw? I think back over the past few days. When did I first see her? It was in the barn I realise but no one else was there. Buster wasn't there, was he?

The second time I thought I saw her in the garden…I haven't told anyone about that. The next time was here, right here, I realise. I stand up and walk to the fireplace, my hand going to the shelf where I placed the card yesterday. I look towards the sofa, half expecting to see Beatrice curled up on the cushions, hugging Buster. It is empty. Christmas Eve, where would she be? Of course, she went to the barn didn't she, with her sister? They were looking for the angel. Try as I might, I cannot envisage the tragic scene that I have just read about.

"Ah, there you are!" Gran has found me and is holding out a cup of hot chocolate, "here, join us in the sitting room, your mum has made some mince pies, they are delicious!" Her bright smile could be hiding any manner of things. I know my Gran, she will stay positive through everything (thank the lord).

I am reluctant to let go of the book but I leave the diary on the table and follow her into the sitting room. It is remarkable that Becky has baked those mince pies. As a rule, back home, she never seems to have time to put more than a ready meal in the oven. She has done us proud. I take my place on the sofa, between Gran and Joe and for the time being put all thoughts of Beatrice and the diary out of my mind.

"You still getting those feelings of deja-vu?"
I stare at Gran. I don't recall saying anything about the odd feelings I have been getting, that I have been here before. She is giving me one of her knowing looks though.

"Deja-vu?" That's Becky, "You didn't tell me, Hannah," she accuses.

"Well, they haven't happened much and everyone gets them, don't they?" I want to make light of the situation because, to be honest, I have not yet worked out how serious or inconsequential anything I might say or do, could be.

"Well, I don't think I have been here before," George laughs, trying to follow my lead.

Gran doesn't say anything else, though I feel she wants to.

"Where does Mrs Carmichael live?" I try to sound as though it is of no real interest to me, as though it is of no consequence whether I find out or not.

"You'd best ask your Gran," Becky says, "I am not sure but I think she lives in the village, that's what she said isn't it?"

I look at Gran who is, it must be said, looking a tad sheepish,

"Well, yes, of course I know where she lives. We may not have seen as much of each other as we'd have liked over the years but we have kept in touch and we used to spend a lot of time together as children."

I stare at Gran. If Mrs Carmichael is her cousin then we are related. I ponder this for a while but it doesn't answer my original question. Gran seems to realise this.

"She lives in the village…Primrose Cottage, pretty little cottage opposite the church. It's about a mile away from here. Not thinking of going there are you?"

I shake my head.

"I was just interested, because of the diary, I wanted to give it back to her but maybe after Christmas," I fib.

"I like the name," I say, casual indifference in my tone I hope, rather than the pent up excitement of anticipation that I am feeling right now. Gran throws me a strange look. I avoid her eye.

"It's a lovely afternoon, I might go and explore…" I tell them after a while. Everyone looks at me as though I am mad. The sky hangs heavy with threatened snow.

"It's Christmas Eve," Becky objects as though that alone precludes any idea of leaving the house.

"Some fresh air will be good for you, you are looking a bit pasty," puts in Gran. I hope she isn't going to suggest

165

she comes with me, that would never do. I send her a grateful smile.

"Well, stay close to the cottage, no gallivanting across those fields – the drifts could be quite deep…and take your mobile with you. Just in case," Becky adds, at my look of distain. I pick up my phone which has no signal of course and head to the kitchen to don my boots and coat. I pick up my scarf and gloves too, that sky does look rather grey.

"Don't be too long!" calls Becky from the other room. Gran winks at me. The clock on the kitchen wall chimes one and a cherub pops out. It really is a very ugly clock, I think. I cannot imagine why it is there. Maybe Mrs Carmichael didn't want it in her own house. It doesn't even keep time very well. I wouldn't blame her.

The diary is tucked into the inside pocket of my coat. It is quite small. I pat it to ensure it is still there. Then I leave the cottage and wave at Gran as she closes the door. She continues to watch from the window as I walk down the path, to the road. As I turn the corner I am out of view and breathe a sigh of relief. The road has been cleared again and gritted. Despite this, my progress is slow because I slip and slide a fair bit until I reach the end of the lane. Here I stop. Which way? I think we came in from the right the other day but it is hard to tell because the road signs were covered. I read them aloud.

"Little Minton 1 mile, Under Minton 3mls," Well, we didn't drive through a village on the way here so I think it is worth trying Little Minton. A mile isn't very far. Of course, a mile in the snow is another matter as I soon find.

I am half way along the road to Little Minton when the post van passes me. It pulls up by a half buried post box some way ahead and its driver jumps out to empty the box.

"Excuse me!"

He doesn't hear. I am sure he will have driven away before I reach him. I quicken my step, and call again, "Excuse me!"

He is loading the bag back into the van and locking the box. I begin waving my arms about in manic fashion, calling as I do so. At last, he turns and puts his hand to shade his eyes against the brightness of the snow. He waits as I half run, half stagger, towards him,

"You ok?"

"Yes, fine thank you but I am looking for a cottage…Primrose Cottage," I explain, "I think it is in Little Minton," A postie will know won't he?

"Primrose Cottage eh?" he scratches his chin, "that'd be the red brick cottage opposite the church," I am pleased I am on the right track.

"You are going the right way but there is a quicker path, through the church yard. It's just the other side of that. Avoids the main road." I thank him, I hadn't noticed the spire in the distance but now that he points it out I can see the footpath and I am grateful to take it. The path is obviously well trodden, someone has gritted it and there is less chance of falling given the railings standing either side to hang onto. I make my way slowly but safely up to the church.

A choir is singing as I approach, Christmas carols echo across the churchyard. I feel sad because this is so perfect and Becky and George and Gran are missing it. I consider going back to get them or calling them…I glance at my phone. There is a signal here, faint it is true. I almost make the call but then I remember why I have come here. I use the phone take a shot of the church and the ethereal light, that floods the snow covered churchyard. I will show them that instead.

Determined, I trudge on, my feet crunching into the snow at every step. I emerge from the churchyard, by a row of white washed cottages their thatched rooves now covered in snow. To the left of those, stands a small, yet imposing, red brick house, Primrose Cottage, set behind ornate, iron railings. It looks as though it has been plucked straight from a fairy tale, Gran got that much right. There is a light in the window at the front. I check my watch. 2 o'clock. It has taken me an hour to get here.

I consider my next move. Should I just march up to the front door and ring the bell, ask for Mrs Carmichael…but then what? Do I ask if Beatrice is dead? Mrs Carmichael has her diary, that could mean Beatrice was her daughter couldn't it? It seems insensitive to ask such a question but why would she give that diary unless she wanted me to ask questions? Perhaps she too has seen the ghosts.

I check my watch again. If the diary is correct then I have more than enough time to get back to the cottage and do whatever it is that the little girl is asking me to do.

I take my courage in both hands and push open the wrought iron gate. It creaks on its hinges and I expect someone to peer out of the window at any moment but no one hears. Across the way, the voices peel out, The Holly and the Ivy, I swallow hard. Get a grip Hannah! I take a few steps along the path. Still no one appears to have noticed me so I walk right up to the shiny black front door with its Festive Holly wreath, and lift the brass knocker, letting it clatter against the wood.

Before the noise of the knocker dies away, I hear footsteps. I consider the option of turning tail and running but that would be ridiculous. I am not doing anything wrong am I? I stand my ground and wait.

Chapter twelve

Beatrice

To say I am surprised to see the girl, would be an understatement. I had not realised she would track me down. I did not think she would be that curious. I had hoped the diary would make her realise the importance of today but she is not supposed to be here, she is meant to be in the barn. For a dreadful moment, I see all the years of planning and searching coming to nothing. What irony that would be! I check my watch, 2pm. It is not time yet. If it is meant to be...I hear Nick's warning words ringing in my brain as I open the door.

"Hannah!" I say, trying to sound calm and non plussed when I am anything but. As for Hannah, she looks what? Frightened? Anxious? Excited? It is difficult to tell. Cold, she looks cold, I decide. I remember my manners,

"Do come in out of the snow," I smile.

"Well, I am sorry to bother you Mrs Carmichael but I have some questions, about the diary and I thought, this being Christmas Eve, it would be a good time to ask you."

I set a cup of hot chocolate in front of my ghost girl and invite her to warm up by the fire. She seems grateful. I take a deep breath,

"Questions? Better ask them then," I suggest, trying to keep my voice low and even. I don't think I am doing a very good job because she is looking at me oddly.

"Only if you are sure it's ok," she replies.

"Ask away," I assure her.

"Well, I read the diary this morning, after you left. The thing is, I have to ask, is Beatrice dead?"

The question so unbalances me I almost laugh. She hasn't guessed then.

"No, not at all," I say eventually.

"Well," a puzzled look crosses her face, "The thing is, I have seen a girl, a girl who I thought could be Beatrice, in the cottage but if she is still alive then that can't be right."

"You saw Beatrice today?" I am holding my breath for her reply, this is not how I remember it. If she saw me in the cottage, that is news to me. I don't recall seeing her. It is too good to let pass,

"Not today, no, yesterday, in the snug, she was reading, she had a dog on her lap…"

I bite my lip…she saw Buster? It's a strange emotion that runs through me then. Buster lived to a ripe old age but she got to see him yesterday? I am almost jealous but then I pull myself together. This is happening and it is happening now. I must keep focused.

"Would you like to see a photograph of Beatrice?" I ask. She nods. I reach up and take down the group photo that sits on my mantelpiece.

"This is she," I smile.

The girl stares at the photograph for a moment. The black and white print does not detract from Mary's beauty or the probable redness of her hair. We girls sit with an arm around Nicholas in the middle.

"But that's the girl I saw, that's Beatrice?"

I need to tread softly now. She has pieced together so much but there is the important part now. I take the photograph from her.

"Yes, that's Beatrice. That is me," I tell her.

"You? But, if you are Beatrice why did I have to read the diary? Why couldn't you just tell me all this?"

"Because you would never have believed me and your parents would have thought I was mad and because, this is the way it had to be." I raise my hands in apology but really, what else could I have done?

Rachel and I discussed it hour after hour. How could I let her know what happened that day without frightening her, without spoiling everything? We knew I could leave it all to play out. Hannah would go into the barn and she would see us and she would let Buster in…and the gun would fire. At what point could we change things? How am I to explain this before it is time?

She is struggling with this revelation. That much is clear because she is staring at me as though trying to connect me with that long ago me, the one she saw yesterday.

"You were the little girl sitting on the sofa with Buster. So, that means, if you are not a ghost, I saw you as a child?"

"Yes, that's right. I was twelve years old,"

"I thought you were younger than that when I saw you the first time,"

"Old fashioned clothes!"

"But, you seemed to see me?"

"I did, I saw you then and again in the garden and then again, in the barn…"

"So, that really happened? The gun firing and your sister dying? But that is so sad!"

I see tears well up in her eyes and I realise that she still doesn't realise the enormity of what she has been told. There is nothing for it, I must explain everything. I pull out the photograph that Rachel found, the one from the Box Brownie, with Hannah in the background. I don't want to spook the girl too much but, she needs to see it. She is quiet for what seems an eternity.

"I was there," she breathes.
I smile,

"No Hannah, you will be there, in your world, that moment hasn't happened yet,"

We sit there, puzzling over this impossible statement for a while before she speaks again,

"Tell me all of it," she says.

When I have finished, the clock shows that it a quarter to three.

"So, you think by going into the barn today, I can change what happened? But that's crazy,"

"Crazy is us having met in 1963 don't you think? Crazy is that we are second or third cousins."

She shakes her head. For one so young, she seems to have grasped this better than I had hoped.

"What time did it happen?" her small voice jolts me out of my musing.

"The accident? 4 o'clock." I remember the church clock chiming four just as Mary took that Photograph, seconds before…

"So, you think I could change what happened? But how? By not going into the barn at all?"

I had thought of that. It would be easy to suggest she stays here for an hour or so, let the time pass, see what happens. It is one of the first options that Rachel and I came up with in those long discussions over a bottle of wine and a pizza. We discounted it because although Buster came into the barn when the door was opened by Hannah, maybe he could have got in anyway. It will be better to have someone there, to make certain. Besides, if we change too much, then what will this do to Hannah? We have to let her follow the original plan to some degree. Nicholas and I came to that conclusion a long time ago.

"Some things have to happen as they did; you staying away might not change anything."

"So, you don't blame me?"

"Blame you? Good heavens no," I am horrified at the suggestion, "For one thing, we don't know how or why you appeared. Perhaps it was us who called you there. We just don't know so to change things so much, might not work at all."

"And what do you think will happen to me?" this is a smaller voice.

The question has vexed me for some time. What will happen to Hannah? Part of me believes she is here now and will still be here afterwards but suppose, just suppose that she isn't, what will that mean for her and her family? I know they have gone through some tough times but they have come through those haven't they? Am I being selfish? This possibility is not lost on me. Do I have the right to expect anything from this twelve year old child, whose eyes are now boring into mine? I won't risk more than I need to. I am honest.

"I don't think anything will happen to you because your Gran, Rachel was not with us that day. Your Mum and Dad had their own lives, nothing to do with us. You being here does not depend on whether or not Mary survives but I can't promise anything, Hannah, do you understand?"

She takes her time and nods,

"I think so. In your world, I go back in time whether or not I want to. I mean, I didn't do anything that I know of, to get myself back yesterday…so me going into the barn will happen whatever I do because it has already happened…"
I see her thinking, struggling with this ridiculous conundrum. Should I mention the clock's possible part in all this? I decide against it. Some things must be left to fate.

"So, it is your family's past that could change. You and my Gran would still be cousins and Joe and I will still be born…will we even be at the cottage this Christmas?"

"I think so," I pause, "I don't know, Hannah," I have no more answers, this is as far as my long and sometimes painful search, has taken me.

She seems to sense my sudden inability to think and becomes brisk,

"Well, it's simple as I see it. I go back to the cottage and if I go into the barn and see you three playing…I will make sure that Buster doesn't come in. That's all?"

"That's all," I say, with a helpless shrug.

"It seems such a small thing,"

"It was just a small thing, but crucial," my voice shakes.

I am less than convinced now than I have been. Should we tamper with what has already been done? Maybe Hannah goes into the barn and doesn't see any of us. Maybe someone else opens the door and lets Buster inside in this altered world? I am getting ready to drop the entire idea. Never has it seemed so outlandish. I am about to tell her not to worry, let's just forget all about it. I reckon without Hannah's stubbornness.

"Well, if I have to get back for 4 o'clock, I might need a lift?" she suggests.

Chapter thirteen
Hannah

Mrs Carmichael has surprised me. That's for sure. I had no idea that she is the Beatrice I have been seeing as a child. Of course, now I know, it is easy to see the likeness, but I would have put that down to her being a daughter or a sister. Mrs Carmichael, Beatrice, is desperate. I could see that the moment she started speaking even though she tried to hide it. I suppose I was doing the same. Funny, but if my life changed would it matter so much? I have told the psychiatrist often enough that I sometimes feel my life is worthless. Becky and George would doubtless carry on bickering and Gran, would she be sorry if I had not been born? She'd never know of course. The possibility hangs before me. Maybe I'd have different parents. That idea is quite a novel one. I push it away of course, Despite their ineptness as parents, I do have feelings for Becky and George, feelings which have come more to the fore since we arrived at Angel Cottage. Is that significant? Perhaps. Then there is Joe of course. I can't help wondering though, what if?

I stare at Beatrice for what feels like a lifetime and what might very well turn out to be just that. She is faltering, I can tell. I want to know more. I want to know everything. What has life turned out like for her and her family? How did she find me? How did she know it would be me? I think I know but perhaps I have no idea at all. The diary stopped short of anything that happened after that Christmas.

I glance at my watch. It is already gone 3pm. I have no idea how I will manage to avoid my family and sneak into the barn. By now, they might be out looking for me. I feel a stab of guilt.

"Do you want to let your mother know where you are?" I am taken aback. A few short days ago I'd have said no, because in all honesty, Becky would have been so high on whatever she had taken, she would not have noticed my absence. George might have, it depended on how he felt. If he had one of his headaches, he'd be lying in a darkened room, dead to the world.

I take out my mobile and see that there is a message sitting there. It is from Gran. She wants to know if I am ok. I tap a reply and put it back in my pocket.

"Gran will let them know," I tell her.

"Your Gran is a lovely lady," she says.

"Yes," I say, somewhat surprised, "she is," I wonder how she and Gran could have been so close yet I feel I have only just met this woman.

I sense that Beatrice might call everything off given half the chance. She is more worried than she first let on. If there is anything to rationlise here, it is that I have to go back to the cottage with my family and, whatever happened in 1963, I am likely to witness it. I can't say the thought of witnessing someone being shot, is appealing but right now, I don't think about that, I only think about stopping something happening. It isn't as though I have to do much is it? It is decided.

Stepping out into the snow again, I am struck by the bizarre normality of it all. The choir have finished their recital and people are filing out of church, laughing and joking. A family with two small children are throwing snowballs at one another, a Golden Retriever is rolling in the snow with abandon, ecstatic to find such fun. It is like a scene from a Christmas card. I have to stop to take it in. Do I want this to be changed? Will it be changed? Too late, I have made up my mind. Besides, it is possible that nothing might happen at all. I hope that Beatrice won't be too disappointed in that case. She must have got used to life without Mary by now.

"Jump in," Beatrice has opened the passenger door on her red Golf. I climb in and pull the seat belt towards me. It is such a normal thing to do. Normality is all around. Beatrice drives slowly along the lane. The mile journey takes a few minutes as she takes care to avoid the ice and the ruts but we arrive just after 3.30pm. Beatrice doesn't pull into the drive. She doesn't want anyone to notice us.

"You know what to do?" she is nervous now. I nod.

The lights twinkle behind the curtains of the cottage. I am glad they are closed. I am glad no one is standing outside waiting for me.

"You had better go in and tell them you are home," Beatrice says after a few minutes.

"But what if they stop me from going into the barn?"

"They won't, something sends you there. I don't know what but you came, back then. Go and see."
She virtually pushes me out of the car and I watch her drive away. I can only imagine her feelings right now, leaving me to her fate as it were.

I push open the back door and stamp my boots on the mat.

"Oh, there you are! We were about to send out a search party," laughs Gran. Becky is rolling pastry again. Will wonders ever cease? This is strange, very strange, are things already beginning to change? Is it too late to back out now even if I wanted to?

Behind me, I hear something banging.

"It's that damned barn door again! Keeps banging, we've shut it twice. Would you be a love and go close it again please Hannah, before you take your coat off?" George is peering out of the window. "Maybe there's a window open in there. Maybe I should go and look…"

177

I shake my head, "It's ok Dad, I'll go. I'll check the window too,"

"Can't argue with that, looks a bit chilly out there!" he grins and goes back to his crossword puzzle. Crossword puzzle? What's all that about? I look at them all. Better try and commit this to memory just in case. Just in case of what? Well, in case I cease to be for some reason or things are different. I want to remember this, how it is, right now. The fact that if I cease to be I won't be able to remember at all is lost on me at this point.

I look across at Becky, flour all over her skirt, laughing and joking with Gran who is scrubbing something in the sink, Dad doing his crossword.

"Well, if you're going, go before it gets dark," laughs Gran. Is there an edge to her voice? Does she sense an urgency? I try to slow the thudding of my heart by deep breathing, in through the nose, out through the mouth…

"Won't be long," I say as I open the door, my heart now beginning to thud out of control. The clock on the kitchen wall might be slow I realise. It says ten to four but suppose it is later? I check my watch. Ten to four. I have ten minutes.

"I'll be ten minutes," I say.

"To shut a door?" they chorus.

I laugh,

"Going to check the window and there's something in there I want to look at, won't be long," I say as nonchalant as I can be.

The door closes behind me and a subtle change occurs as I cross the yard. Is the snow deeper? Is the barn light on? I can hear voices.

Something brushes my ankles, Buster! I bend down and make a fuss of him and he follows me. I realise my mistake. Buster must not accompany me into the barn. I look around and see his yellow ball, sitting on the rain butt.

I pick it up and whistle. His ears prick up and he watches as I raise my arm. As I near the barn door, I throw the ball as far as I can so that he is running, joyful in the chase, towards the cottage.

I don't wait to see whether he gets the ball, I heave the door open and step inside, pulling it closed behind me. I hear Buster barking somewhere on the other side. Unsure of what I should do next, I turn to the sound of voices and look up.

The children are there, all three of them. Seeing them as a family for the first time, I feel my blood run cold. I have not seen any except Beatrice until now. Those were glimpses of a girl from another time, in the barn, in the garden and in the cottage. Beatrice and Buster. This is my first sighting of the other two children. I am aware that I have been holding my breath and I let it out in slow gasps. I study the tableau before me.

Beatrice is pulling on a woollen poncho and Mary is winding on the film in an old fashioned looking camera. Nicholas is strutting around in a bowler hat and stops when he comes to a creaky floorboard. He presses the board experimentally with his foot. It squeaks, he does it again and then bends to investigate. Beatrice has turned and is staring straight at me, her eyes wide as they lock with mine.

"Hey smile!" Mary presses the shutter and laughs. I realise that this is the photograph that I will be in. Beatrice is still staring at me, frozen in her pose. I smile encouragement and step back into the shadows as Mary presses the shutter again.

Nicholas is calling the girls,

"Look what I found!"

I can't see from here but I know all too well what he is holding up

"Put it down!" chorus the girls, as one.

I cannot breathe. Have I done enough? To say time stands still, sounds, silly, a tired cliché, but it does, it really does. There is no future. There is no past and at this moment, the present hangs by a thread. Somewhere in my head I can hear the ticking of a clock, it stutters and ticks too fast, then stops…My own heart is beating fast as I stare at those children from a time before I was born, yet as alive now as I am.

"It's a gun!" screams Beatrice. Nicholas is holding it aloft. It is heavy, he stumbles a little under the weight. Will he drop it? Buster isn't there, Nicholas struggles to regain his balance and takes a step forward. The gun wavers in his hands.

"Put it down!" they cry again and as I watch, Nicholas regains control of his find for a moment, managing to lower it, gently, to the floor.

Time seems to adjust itself and I let out an audible gasp which is drowned by the shouts of the children,

"Quick, leave it there and go and get Dad!" Mary is ordering, "Come on, let's get out of here,"

Three pairs of footsteps echo across the loft floor. I shrink as far back as I can, into the shadows as they file down the ladder, breathless. Mary, red headed and bossy, Beatrice, brown haired and determined, Nicholas, sandy haired with a cheeky grin that has been wiped from his face as he realises the enormity of what just happened. Once down, they turn and race for the door, already yelling for their parents.

I stand and stare for what seems an eternity. Should I leave now? If I stay, will I see more? I am curious to know what happens next. I am considering my options when I see that I don't have a choice. My job is perhaps done, if there was a job to be done. Things have changed again. The change is almost imperceptible. The light is no longer on.

The window upstairs is open again, the barn door is banging. I flick on the light and climb those steps in a trance, crossing the floor and pulling the errant window closed with a bang. This time it catches. As I step back, my foot lands on the loose floorboard. A shiver runs the length of my spine. I look down. My foot presses the board and makes it squeak just as Nicholas's did moments before. Bobbing down, I feel round the board's rough, splintered edges and pull. It lifts with little effort. It must have been moved in my time as well as in theirs then. I am relieved to find that no gun lies there, just a brown cardboard box. It is feather light. I take off its lid and pull out the Christmas Angel.

I replace the board and tread it down. I carry the angel down the stairs, careful not to crush her. Once downstairs, I switch out the light and close the barn door.

The yard is empty. No dog, no deep snow, just the few inches that fell earlier. Our car sits on the far side, by the fence.

"Done it? That was quick," Gran says as I walk back into the kitchen.

I feel as though I have been gone ages. I smile at her.

Nothing seems to have changed. I feel vague disappointment. What had I expected? Becky is putting a tray of sausage rolls into the oven, George is re-kindling the fire. Joe has appeared and is listening to his music with his headphones on.

I feel dizzy with relief. It is all the same. I am sure of it. I run up to Gran and give her a hug.

"Happy Christmas," I say.

"What about us?" I stare at Becky and George and in that instant, I realise that they cease to be Becky and George, they have become Mum and Dad. Is it all the same? I am less sure now. My mind feels as though it is erasing a bad memory and when I do realise what that bad memory is, I understand.

"Beatrice, Ray and her brother Nick are coming over this evening, I thought it'd be nice to have a few drinks. She has been so kind and I haven't seen Nicky for ages. That's if they can get through the snow,"

"Oh, they can," I say, getting strange looks in return. Beatrice and Nick, coming to see Mum and Dad? It is a little surreal.

"What about Mary?" I can't resist asking. The enormity of my question being lost on my parents of course.

"Mary? She will be working, I expect," Dad says.

So, they know Mary as well. I need to get my facts straight. Beatrice will be here soon and she may not remember anything that has happened. Why would she? Why do I? Mary is alive and well, her life seems to have panned out and Mum and Dad seem, normal. It is then that I notice the scar on Dad's head, or the lack of one. I notice he no longer has a limp. Did he not have an accident in this life? I stare at him for a moment. He is standing tall and there is something so normal about him I want to shout out.

"Penny for them," Gran says. At least she is the same I think, but even Gran looks less strained, less on guard…her hair a little less grey.

"Gran," I begin, wondering how to pose this question which might send her into hysterical laughter or me to a psychiatrist. Have I seen one of those already? I don't think I have.

"Yes love,"

"You know when I went out to the barn…"

Gran puts her fingers to her lips and presses them with a wink.

"Life is full of surprises isn't it?" she whispers.

She knows something, she must do. All those questions she asked earlier, she does know.

"Right, they'll be here about seven? I'll time dinner for about half past. The AGA is great, wouldn't mind one myself," Mum (Becky) adds. It is so good of Bea to let us have this place for Christmas."

The familiar way she speaks Beatrice's name confirms it. Things have changed. There is an AGA in the kitchen for a start. I glance at the wall. The angel clock still ticks a little fast. Gran is watching me I realise and winks at me again as she answers her daughter,

"Yes, well, I grew up with Beatrice, we were like sisters being the same age. We've always kept in touch. She's always said we could have the cottage any time, but we haven't got together for a good chin wag for a while," Gran replies with another wink in my direction.
I am confused now.

"Gran, what made you book this place?" I ask.
Becky is checking the oven,
Gran smiles and shakes the cloth out over the table,
"Beatrice suggested it in her Christmas card, I suggested it to your mum and bingo, here we are," she grins.

"Great idea Mum," Becky laughs and I feel a phantom weight being lifted off my shoulders. Am I the one going mad here?

I am staring at my father who is dancing round the kitchen to something he's put on the iPod. As he passes Becky, he grabs her arm and whirls her twice round the table. She allows herself to be thus twirled for a bit before extricating herself and returning to the task of basting the joint.

I search my memories, there was an accident, the day I was born, I know it. Yet, I cannot recall now what happened. I want to ask but would that be weird? I steal another look at my father. No, there is no scar.

"What's up?"

"Oh, nothing, I was just thinking about what might have been, when you know…" I trail off. My mother stands up and looks at my father,

"I know just what you mean, not a day goes by when I don't thank our lucky stars that Mary Grey drove by not a minute after your Dad flew off the road."
She smiles at him and he blows her a kiss.

Mary Grey – that would be Beatrice's sister.

"Amazing coincidence wasn't it?" I push.

"Fate, I call it," George laughs, "Mary says if it hadn't been her, someone else would have come along but her being there, how lucky was that? My very own neuro surgeon no less!"

"No one else would have come along," I say before I can stop myself, "I mean not for ages,"
They all look at me then, a little surprised.

"Now then, why are we talking about the accident? It's Christmas Eve, we are expecting visitors so let's get in the party mood eh?" Gran chivvies us all along and I am left to ponder this new situation I find myself in. The strange thing is, it is feeling less strange by the second. My sense of what is real and what is imagined is diminishing to the point where I can no longer be sure of anything. I am struggling to keep what just happened in the barn in my mind.

"Where's Joe?" I ask, all at once afraid that in this new and carefree world, Joe did not make it for some reason.

"I'm staying clear of you mad lot," says a familiar voice from behind the snug door. I peer round the corner to see him sitting on the sofa leafing through the books on the shelf.

"What's that one?" I ask as he pulls one off the shelf to read,

"Shroedinger's Cat," he laughs, "Quite interesting but completely ridiculous of course – it'd be above your head, Twig, Quantum Theory."

I smile, Twig, he called me Twig, so not everything has changed.

I have stood back and watched for long enough. Now I can join in at last, I realise. The final jigsaw pieces are sliding into place. I wonder how Beatrice is coping.

"Oh, I found this in the barn, we can put it on the tree," I say casually, dropping the Christmas Angel onto the table.

Chapter fourteen

George

November 2000

The journey from Bristol to Lanscott, is tricky. Several roads have been closed due to the sudden snowfall. The Railways have been affected. People are stranded on station platforms up and down the South West. George is due to catch the 5.45pm from Bristol. His wife is expecting their second baby. He is anxious to be there for the birth. She is already several days overdue. This is his last business trip before Christmas. He has promised her that. He will be home tonight. Before he sets off, he rings her.

"Becky? Everything ok? I might be a bit later than planned. The trains have been cancelled. I am going to try and get the last one to Exeter and then grab a taxi…"

"Ok, but they are saying the roads are really bad sweetheart, tell that taxi driver to drive safely," she tells him.

"No twinges?"

"None, this baby is stubborn,"

"Right, I will see you before midnight all being well," he smiles into his phone.

The wind has got up and the snow has become heavy in places. He gets to Exeter station and searches the boards, his train is leaving now. He has to almost leap the ticket barrier to get onto the platform, flashing his railcard at the startled guard as he does so. The train glides to a stop and its doors open. He takes the stairs two at a time.

"Watch out mate!" yells a fellow passenger as he passes. He apologises with a wave over his shoulder and tears along the platform. The doors are closing. He presses the button several times and the guard, noticing him there, takes pity and opens the door so he can board.

"You were lucky, they've cancelled the next one," the guard confides as he checks the railcard. George sinks into the nearest vacant seat and catches his breath. He is a lucky bastard he thinks and closes his eyes…

"Exeter!"

George's eyes snap open. He looks around him. His fellow passengers are moving. Picking up his briefcase, he shuffles along behind them and steps onto the platform.

It is useless to try and hurry. Everyone is eager to get home and he just has to let himself be carried along by the crowd. In the foyer, he is free to make his own way across to the exit. The station forecourt teems with weary travellers. The lucky ones greet family and friends and climb into the warmth of a familiar car. They are the ones who will thank God they remembered to arrange a lift. George didn't have anyone he could ask for a lift. Becky is far too pregnant to be dragged out and she has Joe to contend with too. He is happy to get a taxi. There are no taxis available. There is a hire car firm up the road though, the station Guard tells him. He heads up there.

The car is not a four-wheel drive. He wonders how it will perform on these roads. They don't have any others right now. He could wait, the Boss has taken a four-wheel drive out but is due back in an hour. He is almost tempted but he has promised Becky he will be home. Another hour and the roads may be worse and he might not get through at all. It is already 7.30pm. At least if he goes now, he stands a chance of getting home at a reasonable time. The snow has stopped for a bit but more is forecast. The sooner he makes a move, the better.

"You'll be ok as long as you take it easy. The snow ploughs have been out and gritted the main roads," the chap at the desk assures him as he hands over the keys.

George thanks him and walks across the yard to where the red Vauxhall Astra sits, waiting. He grimaces as he squeezes behind the wheel. Well, it will get him home and Becky can have the baby when she likes then. He throws his briefcase on the backseat and pushes the key into the ignition. A pleasing roar is returned. He revs the engine a little before reversing out of the yard and onto the main road. Out of the corner of his eye he notices the Garmin StreetPilot on the seat. He won't need that. He was born and bred round here.

The roads here have been gritted just as the chap at the car hire firm promised and traffic is moving at a reasonable speed. He switches on the radio which crackles into life. He settles back to listen to the news for a bit before switching channels to something classical. The music washes over him. He feels good. He hums along for a while. The windscreen is misting up, he turns on the heater and watches it clear, the wipers swishing back and forth. It has started to snow again he notices as he reaches the end of the dual carriageway and moves off onto the main road to Lanscott. The gritters have done their job well here. There are fewer cars now, he makes good time.

At 9.15pm he stops in a layby and phones home.

"Yes, we are fine," Becky assures him, "Mum is here, she came over earlier and is going to stay,"

"That's good," he says, relieved that someone is with her. Rachel is sensible, she'll make sure everything is ok. He thinks he has been lucky as far as mother-in-laws go. Some of his friends seem to have picked veritable dragons. Rachel has always seemed, well, nice.

He takes a swig from the water bottle and then moves the car out into the road. Someone ahead of him coming in the opposite direction, flashes their lights at him. He doesn't know why, is he going too fast? He doesn't think so. Are his lights on? He checks. Yes. He turns up the speed of the windscreen wipers. The snow is getting heavy now. He can see next to nothing. He slows right down and sighs. The radio tells him there are blizzard conditions ahead. The car slides on a patch of ice and he slows down even further. He can't see any gritters on this stretch of road. At this rate, he'll be home at Christmas and not before.

A few yards along and he has to slam his foot on the brake. The car swerves and slides to a stop in front of a fallen tree. Woah! That was too close for comfort he thinks. So, that was why the chap was flashing him. Well, lucky, he was going slow.

He looks around. He could try and move the tree but judging by the size of it, you'd need a tractor for that. He reverses the car and turns it round. He'll just have to go another way. He remembers the Garmin and reaches for it. The screen blinks at him and dies.

There is another route home he remembers from summer jaunts. He taps the Garmin again but it fades and gives up the ghost. No matter, he pulls out his phone but there is no signal out here of course. Who would he phone in any case? Not to worry. He should know this place like the back of his hand. He will drive to the next signpost. If he takes the back lanes, he can still get home before midnight he reckons.

He gets out to scrape a pile of snow from the windscreen. The overhanging trees have deposited their load as he sits there. He works out which direction he needs to take. Peering through the dark, he can see the lights of houses to the right, that means the river is to the left. All he has to do is follow the river until he gets to the White Lion, if he remembers, and then take the next right and head due west. It is cross country but with a bit of luck, he can get through. He squints out through the driving snow. Yes, that will work.

The car rumbles through the snow, away from the fallen tree, hugging the river bank until the familiar sign of the White Lion comes into view. It is reassuring to see that there are cars in the car park and lights on in the bar. He is almost tempted to go in for a quick pint or maybe a hot drink but he is conscious of the time. Glancing at his watch he sees that he has wasted enough already. He turns the wheel and the car slides to the right.

The single track slopes down from the main road and winds through the valleys. It would not be his route of choice but with the main road blocked, the luxury of choice has been removed. He manoeuvres the car along the snow-covered track. No gritters have ventured this far, that's for sure. He regrets not having waited for the four by four now. The Astra can barely cope with the snow and slips and slides for the best part of a mile. When the track evens out, he regains some control. He revs the engine and is heartened to hear it still turning over with a healthy roar.

There is a light ahead, is it another car? He isn't sure. He waits but when nothing is forthcoming he decides it is safe to go on.

The light belongs to a tractor. Its driver waves to him. He is clearing the lanes. Good one! he thinks and follows it for some distance. The efforts of the tractor see him right through to Bridley. From here it is just a short trek across country. He is almost home. He thanks the driver of the Tractor who has climbed down and is shaking snow from his hat.

"You be careful up there, mind," the man advises, indicating the rise in the road that he is about to take. He evidently feels the car is far too flimsy to cope.

George thanks him and begins the long haul up the slope. The upper road is well lit but empty of any other cars. It is late, gone ten thirty. Street lamps shine through the snow as he passes through the outlying villages. He makes a sharp left and heads across country towards home.

He is taking it easy, only three miles to go, when the Stag startles him. Leaping over the hedge it stands there staring at him. His instinct is to swerve. The deer blinks and darts away. George thinks how great this will be to tell Joe later, Rudolph blocking his way! He is smiling as he tries to bring the car back from its sudden detour. His hands grip the wheel as it lurches forward, the wheels locking on the icy bank sending the car down, down, into the ditch. The tree branch crashes through the window and his head lolls against the door. A sharp pain, a blinding flash and then, nothing.

A little further along the road, someone is getting into her car to make the short journey to her cousin's house. She doesn't often have the opportunity to have Christmas week off. She is making her usual early, pre-Christmas visit this year and is going to surprise everyone by telling them she will also be here for Christmas Day. She has swapped shifts with one of the consultants. Ulrika wants to travel home to Finland in the new year and was happy to trade places.

She takes the upper road as it is well lit and makes the sharp left turn that will bring her within a stone's throw of her cousin's lane. The four by four she drives, grips the road with ease. She is listening to a podcast. Her mind is elsewhere. The deer that veers across the road as she rounds the bend, startles her but does no harm. She stops for a minute to watch the splendid creature dance across the snow-covered fields, disappearing into the woods. Being here now has already proven fortuitous. Bea has told her she will get to see all the family this weekend. There will be a big gathering at the cottage. Marjorie and Charles, elderly now but still enjoying life, will be there.

Mary is looking forward to it, not least because if they are all in one place, she won't have to make lots of short trips to see them all.

She restarts the engine and keeps her eyes peeled for any more errant deer that may be about to run across her path. She is hoping that her husband, also a surgeon, will get home in time to spend Christmas with her but that's another story. The street lamps make the snow sparkle, she is driving through a fairyland. She smiles at the prettiness of it all. She might take a photograph if she can pull over somewhere. She is considering doing this when she sees a beam of light shining upward, ahead. There is something wrong about the angle. She frowns. An upturned headlight maybe? She forgets about stopping to take a photograph and pushes the car forward.

Rounding the bend, she hears a piercing scream which she later realises is a radio, off frequency. Headlights shine up into the sky. The tangled metal she sees as she draws closer, is a red car. The accident could have happened just seconds before, the wheels are still spinning. It is hard to see how it has ended up here when the road is so well lit. Skidded perhaps? Going too fast? She doesn't stop to consider too much. She is out of the car and scrambling down the bank.

Her phone is in her hand and she is speaking into it even as she reaches the driver, trapped inside.

"RTA Wooten's Corner, High road, possible head injury…air ambulance," she shouts into the phone, pocketing it and flashing her torch at the driver. He has hit his head, there is a slight swelling behind his eyes – she knows time is of the essence. She pulls her medical bag from her shoulder and opens it. Must relieve the pressure as soon as she can…

By the time the air ambulance arrives, George is breathing well and stands a good chance of a permanent recovery. Strapped to the stretcher, he manages to raise his hand to the female knight in shining armour who came to his rescue. She has bright red hair, swept back into a pony tail and looks very familiar. He closes his eyes and the image fades.

"I will get word to his wife," she tells the crew, "Yes, I know her, she's my second cousin,"

So, it is Mary who knocks on Becky's door and imparts the news that there has been an accident but George is ok. They will just need to keep him in for a bit. He will be fine though. It was so lucky she happened to be on the same road. So lucky that she is a Doctor. Everyone will say so afterwards when George is nursing his injuries and joking about the Christmas Stag. Without doubt, her experience in neuro surgery saved him from more permanent injury.

As she takes in the news that George has been hurt, Becky feels her womb contract. She rubs her bump with a rueful wince. The shock of first seeing Mary at her door and then of hearing about the accident, may or may not be responsible.

Rachel sits on the sofa and cuddles Joe who has been woken up by all the noise. Mary offers to drive Becky to the hospital. Becky thinks this would be best, particularly as the shock seems to have brought on labour.

George is drowsy but conscious when they arrive. He waves a feeble arm and says, "sorry," Becky is just grateful he is alive but she cannot hang around for long, the baby has decided to come now.

Chapter fifteen

As I drive away, I find tears welling up in my eyes. I feel a subtle shift in the atmosphere, just a slight change. Can I hear a clock ticking, or is it just my imagination? Something is already beginning to happen, I know it. Just Hannah knowing what she must do, seems to have made a difference. Maybe intent is enough. I don't hang around to find out what will happen here. I must get back. Ray and Nicky are waiting for me. I want to make sure we are together before anything unexpected can happen. I am all at once afraid. For two pence, I would dash back and tell Hannah not to bother, to stay away, but then, everything is outside my control now. I realise that. Was it ever in my control? Nick was there of course, when Hannah knocked on the door. He was tactful and left us alone. We have worked towards this moment for so long and Rachel has been sure for even longer than I that Hannah is the one. Funny how Rachel was the first to guess my ghost girl was her granddaughter. The photo turning up was the proof of course.

I press the accelerator and steer my car into the drive. I can see the church clock, its face reversed in mirror. Mirror, Mirror… It's almost four o'clock.

I can see Nicholas standing by the window. Ray must be inside somewhere. I wave and Nicholas waves back. Our eyes lock. The hands move. I feel a little light headed but after all the excitement that's to be expected. It means nothing, I tell myself. I jump out of the car and run to the door, turning the key in the lock as the hands move again. I am standing in the living room with Ray and Nicholas as the clock strikes four.

As the last chime rings out, I pinch myself to make sure I really am still here. It is now past 4 o'clock, the gun has either fired or not fired, the cat is either dead or alive. There can be no more second chances, no more promised cracks in time. We have arrived.

The snow seems to have stopped. That's good. All this snow is unsettling. It is so reminiscent of that afternoon. I laugh at myself, what afternoon am I referring to? For goodness sake, I remember it so clearly now, the afternoon that Nicholas found the gun. I close my eyes for a moment, letting the memories flood through me. Somewhat jumbled, they seem to be falling into place like a jigsaw that has been put together wrong for so many years, the pieces only now, finding their rightful places. I open my eyes and exhale.

Nicholas is staring at me. A sudden panic comes over me. Where is Ray?

"Are you ok?"

Ray's voice fills me with relief and I throw my arms round him as he comes back into the room with a mug of tea. He laughs and ruffles my hair,

"Watch it, I almost threw it all over you," he laughs, setting the cup down on the table, "There you are madam, thought you might need it,"

Why does he think I might be in need of tea? Does he remember? I check myself, what am I talking about? Panic sets in then. Am I the only one who remembers the old life but does not yet remember the new? Am I now to go mad? I take a deep breath and sit down.

"What time is Mary getting here tomorrow?" Ray asks the question as though it is the most normal question in the world and it is, I realise. It is.

"This'll be the first Christmas Day she's had off since that year George had his accident, won't it?" he continues, picking up the remote to turn on the television.

He is right. We rarely see Mary at all at Christmas but this year she has managed to get Christmas day off and to be in this country. She can't make the drinks and meal tonight but she'll be here tomorrow. Hannah can meet her, I realise and then laugh at myself. Hannah has met Mary many times hasn't she? She is her Godmother after all. It seemed fitting, Becky said, after the accident. I must be going mad.

I study Nicholas who has said little in the last few minutes. I can't imagine what has changed for him. Has anything changed? I build up the courage to ask with a little trepidation.

"Nick?"

"You too?" he says, a wariness in his tone.

"It worked," I say in a whisper that only I can hear, or so I think. Ray raises an eyebrow. You were thinking that something terrible might happen?" he asks. I can only nod. Things have turned out just as I hoped, just as Rachel and I hoped, all those years ago after the gun was found. I don't know what might have happened had Hannah not played her part today. I want to ask her what she saw. To me, she has always been that ghost girl in the shadows. I knew that we'd meet for real one day, ever since Rachel and I discussed her that long ago Christmas. True, I was as amazed as anyone when it turned out she was Becky's daughter but that just made it easier to see how she came to be there that day. Of course, I have never told her anything about it, not until today when I took the diary round. I pause in my thoughts, did I take the diary round today? Did we really sit here in this very room and have that conversation? I am gratified to remember that we did. There is a diary, I did write everything down.

I wait for more memories to flood in and am a little sad to find that I am losing many. I notice a briefcase sitting by the sofa. It is Nicholas's of course. He must have finished lecturing and come straight here.

"So, are you going to ask her what she saw?" Nicholas's question interrupts my train of thought and I must look startled because he grins. I shrug,

"I think she will tell me, I won't have to ask," I decide.

Before I can say anything more, the phone rings. It is Rachel.

"Bea? Look, everything is OK there isn't it?"

"Yes, yes, I think so…" I am no longer sure what I had expected to happen but something has changed, "And there? Is Hannah all right?"

"She did it," Rachel says.

"Yes, I know,"

"She's fine, I think she would like to talk to you about it though,"

"Of course, it's amazing eh?"

"Amazing, see you later then,"

With that, we end the rather stilted conversation and I drop the phone back into its holder. Nick touches my arm.

"I feel as though I have just woken up from a nightmare," Nick tells me, his face a little flushed and his eyes over bright. I nod,

"Me too," I look at Ray. He is pulling the curtains to and switching on the lamps, apparently oblivious to our conversation.

I know she has done it. I hug the knowledge to myself, aware that it could be fleeting. I am living on the cusp of something amazing that I am not sure I will ever appreciate. I grab pen and paper and begin to write. I write as though my life depends upon it. Ray and Nicholas leave me to it. They are used to me getting an idea and scribbling it down. I have a shelf of books in the study that began in this way. Now, I write down everything I can remember. I feel I am floundering at the edge of a vast pool, memories floating away from me as I try to grab at them. I won't give up though. By the time I am finished, I have several sheets of A4 of scribble. I fold it up and push it into an envelope. Tonight, I will let Rachel read it. What will she make of it? The pages contain vague memories of events, beginning with that afternoon in the barn. I glance at the clock. It is 6.30pm.

"Ready?" Ray appears, freshly washed and shaved. He still manages to look as suave as ever and far younger than his sixty-four years. I have tidied myself up and am as calm as I can be as we climb into the car. At least my breathing has returned to normal. Nick jumps in the back and holds all the presents. Ray is driving. I am quiet as he reverses the car into the road. The radio kicks into life and Fairy Tale of New York plays out. Nick says little. It is left to Ray to try and begin a conversation. We are poor companions on the short journey to the cottage.

Memories continue to jump around in my head, rearranging themselves so that I feel quite exhausted by the time we pull into the courtyard. Was I really here just a few short hours ago? Did I set Hannah down and leave her to do whatever it was that she needed to do? I give myself a mental shake. I remember speaking to Mary this morning. I remember saying to Rachel that maybe we needn't do anything. Rachel was sure though. She became sure, the moment we realised that the ghost girl in the barn was Hannah, no maybe before that even.

When I was telling her about the gun, and remembered seeing the girl in the shadows, she said she felt we needed to watch for the girl. She had a feeling that things like this were important. I didn't understand at the time but I wanted to and together, we have tried to fathom out why the ghost girl was so important. It wasn't until Rachel's granddaughter was born, that we knew, beyond a shadow of doubt that Hannah would witness what happened. What difference her presence had made, evaded us. I think we hoped to find out how she came to be there and why. I am not sure that is possible now. Rachel said maybe she was there to warn us, about the gun, like the stories she has heard about ghosts appearing to warn of impending disaster. Have we averted a disaster? Fog clouds my brain and I no longer know what is real and what is imagined. You have a vivid imagination, Beatrice, my English teacher used to say. Rachel was right. We had to let this happen. Of that much, I am sure, very sure.

A memory of another time still lingers on the edges of my mind, as though I have spent half my life, more than half my life, in another era, a parallel universe. I am not sure I can cope with this unsettling sense of being and not being all at once.

I know what I have written down in black and white and these are things that I will not forget. Knowing this does not help me understand.

We walk into the cottage and are greeted by Rachel, Becky, George, Joe and Hannah. I am struck by how beautiful the place looks. They have improved on my meagre attempts at decorations and I have to swallow hard when I see the tree. In pride of place, at the very top, sits the Angel. She found it.

Its significance does not escape me.

Chapter sixteen
1963

It is Christmas Eve, I am twelve years old again. I am chattering to Mary about things that children love to talk about at Christmas. She is parading around in outlandish costumes, I am following suit. She picks up the box brownie and begins to pretend to snap me as though I am a catwalk model. We giggle and preen and the camera shutter snaps shut. I turn and for a moment, I think I see someone standing by the barn door. I stare and she stares back. I am about to call out but something distracts me. Nicholas has found something and is holding it up for us to see. In the dim light, we take a moment to realise what it is he waving about – a gun.

"Put it down!" we yell in unison. He lowers the gun, he falters, it must be heavy, he almost drops it but manages to hold onto it and lays it with care on the dusty boards. Mary orders us out. We shout for our parents, already heading down the steps, all three of us spooked by this thing that has been unearthed. Only as I reach the barn door, do I realise that the girl has gone, if she was ever there.

We are met by our father at the back door, pulling on his boots and about to come and see what the commotion is about. Buster is leaping up at us, furious at having been shut out.

"It's Nicholas, he found a gun, a real gun, look!" I am breathless with excitement, the initial fear having subsided.

"A gun? Where?"

"In the barn, in the barn, it was under the floorboards!" Nicholas is jumping up and down, feeling quite important now that his discovery is apparently of such great interest. Mum appears her hand flying to her mouth as she overhears the word, gun.

"A gun? Charles, be careful, it might be loaded..." she admonishes as our father tells us to stay put and heads off to investigate.

I wonder if he might see the girl but whoever she was, she does only seem to appear to me.

"What was a gun doing in our barn?" Mary asks.

"I have a horrid feeling it was left over from the war...let's see what your father has to say," Mum says, looking a shade whiter than she did just now.

"The war? Do you think Granddad or Uncle Arthur put it there?"

"I don't think so Mary," she is watching with anxious eyes, from the window as Dad makes his way to the barn. He is gone some little time during which we exchange meaningful glances. A gun, a real gun from the war! Who left it there? Is it loaded?

"German gun," Dad says with a surprised air, "You lot have had a lucky escape, it was loaded and ready to fire, don't worry, I disarmed it." Who knew that Dad knew how to disarm a gun? There is a lot we don't know about our parents it seems because Mum is running her hands through her hair, making it fall loose from its hundreds of pins which had held it fast on the top of her head.

"I think I know where it came from..." that's when she tells us the story of the German airman and how he had told her he had hidden his gun in the barn and she had told Grandma Lu but it seemed that either Grandma Lu hadn't been able to find it or she had just forgotten to look because it had lain there undetected for some considerable time. Why he had hidden it was not clear but perhaps he did not want to be seen to be carrying a weapon or maybe he feared being shot and wanted to keep it hidden in case he needed it to escape. We would never know.

"I have called the police station and they are sending someone to pick it up. The desk Sergeant said they are always finding unexploded bombs and devices but no gun as yet, this is the first. I think they will be very interested to hear how it got here, Marjorie?" he is teasing her we realise.

"Charles, be fair, you can't hold me responsible, I was a child, about Mary's age!" she protests, laughing but there is a touch of panic in her voice. It can't be easy to realise that an action of yours, whether inadvertent or not, might have resulted in the loss of your children.

There is a moment in which we all imagine what might have been. During this time, I bring to mind, the image of the girl and I realise, without a shadow of a doubt, that somehow, she helped avoid the tragedy.

I go and find my diary. Nothing ever happens round here but today, something quite amazing has occurred. I must write it down. I might even be able to use it in a story one day. I can imagine the story in my mind's eye. A frightened young German airman drops from the sky over the quiet fields of Devon and a young English girl, helps him to safety. Of course, in my story, the young airman would come back for her after the war and they would marry and live happily ever after. Artistic license would prevail and I might make Marjorie, changing the name of course, a little older, embellish her feelings a little. I wonder if my mother would mind if I did that or if it would upset her.

"What are you thinking?" Mary's voice wakes me from my reverie,

"Oh, just what might have been, that's all," I say.

"Imagine! We could have all be shot or at least one of us could have been killed. Just imagine that for one of your stories Bea, wouldn't that make a good tale? Casting Nick as a murderer... Don't you ever wonder what might happen if just one thing changed, where we would be, what we would do?"

I stare at her for a long time. I take a deep breath and smile,

"I don't need to imagine," I say, "I know,"
And, odd though it may seem, without a shadow of doubt, I do know. As I tell Rachel later when we are visiting her and I find the book on the landing, life would be very different indeed.

Christmas morning sees us all in our pyjamas, opening the presents that have been left beneath the tree. Not a one of us still believes in Santa but the magic is there.

My favourite present is from Mary. The little box, wrapped in paper with holly leaves all over it, opens to reveal a red and gold fountain pen. It is beautiful. I can't wait to use it.

"For your novels!" she beams and I hope she likes the photo frame that I got her, just as much. I have put the photograph of Gilbert inside.

I am writing the final page of my diary. Mary has just had a phone call from Gilbert and is mooning over his photo, now in its frame, in our bedroom. I am amazed at how long she can spend just staring at him.

"It's her age," Mum says and laughs. I imagine Mum as a girl, mooning over the young airman. I rcad part of her diary when Mary found it in the trunk. She was quite taken with him by her own admission. I wonder if Dad was ever jealous but decide it was so long before they met that he could not expect her never to have mooned over anyone else could he? I bet Dad had a few girls he was in love with before he ever met Mum.

Funny to think of one's parents as being young. I suppose they must have been though.

We have to make the most of our time at Angel Cottage. That's the piece of big news to start the new year. We are going to move nearer town so Mary can go to Exeter university once she has her A levels. She is adamant she wants to become a Doctor. Imagine that! We are moving so Mary can train to become a Doctor. No one has asked me where I need to live to follow my dream but I suppose if one wants to be a librarian, any town will do. I can study in town as well as I can here.

Nicholas is not happy about the move, he says he will miss his friends and a new school will be horrible. Mum says it will do him good. He has been getting into trouble at his old school. Mum says it is because he is bored and gets into mischief. Dad thinks a new start will be good for him too.

I will be sad to leave Angel Cottage but I am glad we are not selling it. Mum says she would like to keep it and for now we will let it out, to holiday makers. Mum says the money we make from renting it out, will go some way to paying for our higher education. I don't like to think of strangers going through the rooms and maybe going into the barn. I told Rachel (we are going to stay with her for a while when we move, because the new house is not built yet) She says it will be a shame because she knows all about the ghost girl and everything but then she said something very odd, she said we should try and find out as much as we can about the ghost girl. I can't imagine what she means but it sounds like an idea.

I have documented each time I have seen the girl. I am hoping to see her again before we go but considering I am pretty sure she was here for a reason, and I am not convinced she was a ghost at all, it is not that feasible.

Rachel has promised to visit in the new year, while we are still at the cottage. Auntie Jean has said she can stay with us for a week. Mary is going up to Exeter to check out the new school. It will be good to have some company. Mary just hasn't been the same since she met up with Gilbert. The girl is cuckoo over him!

When Nicholas and I saw her talking to him the other day it made us squirm and when she came home we started singing, "Mary and Gilbert, sitting in a tree, K-i-s-s-i-n-g" until she threw her book at us and poor Gilbert's photo sailed through the air. You should have seen her face! It was as though we had shot him. The photo landed near the fire but I think her hysterical outburst was uncalled for as it didn't go in the fire and she was the one who threw it anyway. Of course, Nick and I got told off but it was worth it just to see her face.

I have overheard our parents talking about Nicholas. He is "a little wayward at times," they say. He needs a firm hand. He will benefit a great deal from his new school which has an emphasis on sport and encourages parental involvement.

Nicholas and I don't have any feelings one way or the other, about the school. We were taken to see it in the Easter holidays and it seemed ok to me. There were lots of pupils running around the school field waving hockey sticks at the time.

"Inter house matches," beams the headmistress. I was glad I was going to be allowed to travel to my old school and would not have to adapt to this new sporting life just yet, if ever.

Nicholas shrugged his shoulders but I could see his eyes light up at the sight of the football pitch. After the undulating hills of our last school field, break a leg if you dare run too fast, this was a revelation. I could see he was itching to get out there with the boys who were kicking a ball around the goal. We viewed the tennis courts and the piece de resistance a swimming pool. It was an outdoor pool but we were told it was heated. Even so, I shivered at the thought whereas Nicholas became alive and talked of little else on the way home.

"I think we have made a good decision with Nicholas," I heard Dad say later, "He might even knuckle down to his lessons at long last," I must say, I do agree with them. Even so, I take a long look at the old barn before we leave. Is that a face I see in the gloom behind the door? I can't be sure. I think I may be imagining it.

We move as the first blossom begins to fall from the trees. It lies like snow upon the ground. The removal lorry is remarkably light as we are leaving most of the furniture. The new house is being furnished from scratch. Even the Angel Clock will stay on the wall. Mum says it is terrible at keeping time but she can't bring herself to throw it out. I suppose it will sit there, ticking away its extra seconds for evermore.

Dad reverses the car out of the drive and as we slide out onto the road, I am puzzled by the feeling of relief that floods over me. The dread of the future which has dogged my way of late, seems to lift. For the first time, in a very long time, I feel light of spirit. I laugh at myself. Am I thinking in clichés now?

Staying with Rachel will be fun I muse. We always seem to have such a lot to discuss. I can't think what, but whenever we meet up, we both feel the need to talk non-stop.

Before we go, I place the Christmas Angel beneath the loose floorboard in the barn. I have no idea why. I am moved to do it by something inside me. Perhaps I want to make sure it stays here.

Chapter seventeen

Hannah 2012

I am grateful that the nightmares have stopped. I am grateful that my parents are normal. I am relieved that Beatrice and her family, my family as it turns out, are safe. However, I can't help wondering whether by changing one thing, there will be consequences down the line.

When I voice these fears to Gran, she tells me that those changes have already occurred and they did have grave consequences, all we have done is set things right again. This keeps me quiet for a while, it satisfies me for a short time. Then I begin thinking again. What if, when I grow up and have children of my own, they too can step back in time? Might they dislodge something, some immutable fact that is in my memory now but might not be in the future.

How do I know that Fate did not mean Mary to die? Suppose she inadvertently causes a world war or the end of the world? Would it have been right to knowingly change things then? The first time, I had no control, no prior knowledge. My presence in Beatrice and Mary's lives was a chance accident as far as I can tell. There was nothing pre-planned about it. Yet, the second time, which was the same time for me (something else that is puzzling me beyond imagination) I knew what might happen if I did nothing so I made sure I stopped the dog from entering the barn. I stopped something happening that had happened, on purpose.

Gran says I am worrying about nothing. She says what has happened has happened but what if she had said that before? Where would we be?

Schrödinger's Cat has a lot to answer for in my book. I keep my copy on a shelf by my bed. When I read it, I imagine Mary, My Godmother, in that barn, waiting for me and it makes me feel better. For over fifty years, she was neither living nor dead. Perhaps we set her free.

Mary became a Neuro Surgeon and she saved my father from certain lifelong injuries. Her quick action on that fateful night, prevented him from suffering life changing brain damage. I am comforted to know that had I not intervened as I did, that would not have happened.
I am so confused that some days, I just sit here and try to work it all out. I have a chart under my bed that follows all the actions we did and could have taken.

I add to it now and then, when something happens that would never have happened had I not been there the second time. That in itself is an oxymoron because it was the first time, the only time, for me. Last month, Mary appeared in the Queen's Honours list. She is getting an OBE for her courageous work. She does a lot of charity work and last year she went out to Sierra Leone and worked with the Aid workers.

I comfort myself with the thought that for that at least she deserves a second chance.
What happened to Gilbert? As first loves often do, this one faded out and Gilbert went off to study economics and then worked in the City. He met a girl, married, had two children, divorced, moved to Spain and now runs a cocktail bar.

I have no doubt that Gilbert has not been affected at all by what happened or didn't happen whereas, Beatrice says that she doesn't remember what happened to him the first time. Was he grief stricken? Perhaps. I tend to think he was shocked and might have cried for a while but otherwise, went on with his life like the rest of us would. Beatrice doesn't seem to worry like I do.

By the time the first buds are showing on the trees, I find the memories are fading fast. Soon, I won't recall how it was before. There will be only now.

Chapter eighteen
Hannah 2000

I am born.

The world has been waiting and I am here, at last.

There are some for whom my appearance represents the culmination of a long and hopeful vigil. I know nothing of their expectations. My focus is on taking my first breath and negotiating my entry into this cold, startling world.

My future is far from being assured. My parents, oblivious to any destiny that may await their only daughter, have scarcely been bothered by my tardy appearance. To be fair, that they have had to wait a little longer than planned for their second child to emerge into the world, is not down to any whim of mine. Birth has its own plan. In some ways, it is a miracle that I ever got myself together enough in the first place.

My father's lengthy absences (he is a travelling salesman) did not make conception easy. If rumour is to be believed, their union was frowned upon by my mother's parents. A travelling salesman whose father had blotted his copy book years before by gazumping them on their very first home, had obstacles aplenty to overcome in winning their approval. But, Hallelujah! I am here.

I am a girl, that much I know. By the look of my mother, I could be round faced and freckled – or are those just the final vestiges of pregnancy that bloat her unremarkable features? I am not smitten by instant love or anything of that sort. I am hungry and looking for food, finding it in her soft, supple nipple, and in the watery, calming liquid that I guzzle like there is no tomorrow. She will squeal in a few hours when I latch on but for now, she is unaware of what is to come.

My father is conspicuous by his absence. He is in the same hospital, attached to a drip, in a bed two storeys above us. He is conscious, a bit bruised but grateful to be alive.

I am pleased that my parents are both receiving the best care but my needs are foremost. I scream for milk and I am given milk. I grizzle and someone cuddles me. I find myself being carried by my mother into the ward where my father is sleeping. He opens his eyes and smiles at me.

"What do we call her," My mother asks, laying me by his side so that he can see me for the first time.

"We should call her Hannah," my father decides. My mother laughs.

"That's nice," she says, "Hannah and Joe, I like it. You gave us all a fright, George. You were so lucky."

"There was a deer you know,"

"A deer?"

"On the road, just before the crash. It leapt out in front of me, just stood there, staring at me for a second. That's when I tried to swerve the car, lost control…"

'What happened to the deer?"

"It just vanished, ran away, I don't know but tell Joe, will you? Santa's reindeer are out and about, I saw one!"

I am here.

Chapter nineteen
Beatrice 2012

It is a cool, winter's day. The January air whips around my shoulders and I pull my scarf more closely to me. We are standing on the hill, overlooking the cottage. From here we can see the whole village spread out before us. The road that winds from the cottage to the church, glints in a wintery sun.

There is not much to say about what has happened now. Nicholas and I have nothing to regret after all. I have a feeling we spent much of our lives working towards something important but the details evade me. Nicholas went to college and got his qualifications. His earlier misdeeds put down to the high jinx of youth, he found his feet and settled down. I sometimes wonder if I have forgotten something that happened in that other past, the one I fought to change for so long. Was my life so very different? There are glimmers of recognition as I go about my everyday life. My memories are real. A childhood, if not idyllic then, happy at least, followed by the trials and tribulations of adulthood. There are no gaps, no feelings of loss. Yet I know something happened to put things back the way they should be. I know this without being told.

I ask Mary if anything has changed in her life recently. There is a fine line between what we know and what we imagine. I feel as though I have woken from a bad dream.

Mary is sitting by the fire with Nick and I. She is just visiting and she thinks about the question and then says something that I think I will always remember, she says,

"The most life changing thing that has ever happened to me was Nick finding that gun and our mother confessing that stuff about the German airman. That shook me up."

"It did?" I am curious now, what can she mean?

"Yes, of course, I mean the gun, war, Granddad being killed in an air raid, Uncle Alfie being wounded, all those poor soldiers who have lost limbs is terrible but it was seeing them that made me know what I wanted to do. I knew I wanted to help people put their lives back together," she gives a short laugh, "I suppose you could say it made me who I am. It's what I do, put people's lives back together isn't it?"

"I can see that," I grin, "I think that day was pivotal for all of us."

Nicholas stares at me and nods. Does he remember anything? I think he does.

In the distance, a cat mews and a dog barks or maybe I am imagining both. Sometimes, often when it is beginning to snow and the air takes on that mystical, quality, I can hear a gunshot somewhere in the recesses of my mind. I can smell the hay and feel the tug of a long-ago time, a time I barely remember now—Once upon a Christmas Eve.

Thank you to my daughter, Zoe McCarthy for interpreting my thoughts and creating the cover design with such insight.

*Erwin Schrödinger was born in Vienna on August 12, 1887 and was awarded the Nobel Prize in Physics in 1933. He is best known for his work regarding quantum theory, particularly about his thought experiment involving a cat in order to explain the flawed interpretation of quantum superposition.

Printed in Great Britain
by Amazon